300

## Back by Po[...]

A collector's edition of six of the most
requested titles from one of the world's
best-loved romance authors. Harlequin
is proud to bring back these sought
after titles in one cherished collection.

### BETTY NEELS:
### RUBY COLLECTION

STARS THROUGH THE MIST

THE DOUBTFUL MARRIAGE

THE END OF THE RAINBOW

THREE FOR A WEDDING

ROSES FOR CHRISTMAS

THE HASTY MARRIAGE

HARLEQUIN®

**Betty Neels** spent her childhood and youth in Devonshire before training as a nurse and midwife. She was an army nursing sister during the war, married a Dutchman, and subsequently lived in Holland for fourteen years. She lives with her husband in Dorset, and has a daughter and a grandson. Her hobbies are reading, animals, old buildings and writing. On retirement from nursing Betty started to write, incited by a lady in a library bemoaning the lack of romantic novels.

Mrs. Neels is always delighted to receive fan letters, but would truly appreciate it if they could be directed to Harlequin Mills & Boon Ltd., 18-24 Paradise Road, Richmond, Surrey, TW9 1SR, England.

## Books by Betty Neels

HARLEQUIN ROMANCE

# BETTY NEELS

## THREE FOR A WEDDING

COLLECTOR'S EDITION

## *Harlequin Books*

TORONTO • NEW YORK • LONDON
AMSTERDAM • PARIS • SYDNEY • HAMBURG
STOCKHOLM • ATHENS • TOKYO • MILAN
MADRID • WARSAW • BUDAPEST • AUCKLAND

ISBN 0-373-83339-3

THREE FOR A WEDDING

Copyright © 1973 by Betty Neels.

This edition published by arrangement with Harlequin Books S.A.

® and TM are trademarks of the publisher. Trademarks indicated with ® are registered in the United States Patent and Trademark Office, the Canadian Trade Marks Office and in other countries.

**Printed in U.S.A.**

# CHAPTER ONE

PHOEBE BROOK, Night Sister on the medical block of St Gideon's hospital in one of the less salubrious quarters of London, raised a nicely kept hand to her cap, twitched it to a correct uprightness, and very quietly opened the swing doors into the women's medical ward. Her stealthy approach to the night nurse's desk might at first glance have seemed to be a desire to catch that young lady doing something she ought not; it was in actual fact, due to a heartfelt desire not to waken any of the patients. She had herself, when a student nurse, done her nights on the ward, and again when she was a staff nurse; she knew only too well that Women's Medical, once roused during the night hours, could become a hive of activity--cups of Horlicks, bedpans, pillows rearranged, even a whispered chat about Johnny failing his eleven-plus, and what would Sister do if she were his mum—so it wasn't surprising that the nurse sitting at the desk put down her knitting and got to her feet with equal stealth, at the same time casting a reproachful look at the clock. She was supposed to go to her dinner at midnight, and it was already half past, and that added on to the fact that she had been alone for the last hour, all of which thoughts Sister Brook read with ease and a good deal of sympathy, even though she had small chance of getting a meal herself. She whispered:

'Sorry, Nurse, I got held up on Men's Medical—a coronary. Come back in an hour.'

The nurse nodded, instantly sympathetic, thinking at the same time that nothing on earth would induce her to take a Night Sister's post once she had taken her finals, and why Sister Brook, with a face like hers, hadn't gone out and got herself a millionaire was beyond her understanding.

She crept to the door, leaving the subject of her thoughts to hang her cape on the chair and lay the pile of papers she had brought with her on the desk—the bed state, the off-duty rota, the bare bones of the report she would have to hand over to the Night Superintendent in the morning—she looked at them longingly, for it would be nice to get the tiresome things done before she left the ward, then she might have time to snatch a cup of tea and a sandwich. But first she must do a round. She went, soft-footed, past the first three beds, their occupants, recovering from their several ailments, snoring in the most satisfactory manner, but the occupant of the fourth bed was awake. Mrs Tripp was elderly and extremely tiresome at times, but the nursing staff bore with her because, having bullied the doctor into telling her just what was wrong with her, she was fighting the inevitable with so much gusto that Sir John South, the consultant in charge of her case, confided to his registrar that he wouldn't be at all surprised if she didn't outlive the lot of them out of sheer determination. Nonsense, of course; Mrs Tripp would never go home again to her ugly little red brick house in a back street near the hospital—she knew it and so did everyone else. The nursing staff indulged her every whim and took no notice when she showed no gratitude, which was why Sister Brook paused now and whispered: 'Hullo, Mrs Tripp—have you been awake long?'

'All night,' said Mrs Tripp mendaciously and in far too loud a voice so that Sister Brook was forced to shush her. 'And now I'm wide awake, ducky, I'll have a. . .'

Sister Brook was already taking off her cuffs, musing as she did so that on the few occasions when she had to relieve a nurse on a ward, she invariably found herself hard at work within a few minutes of taking over. She stole out to the sluice, collecting two more requests on the way, and as all three ladies fancied a hot milk drink to settle them again, it was the best part of twenty minutes before she was able to sit down at the desk.

She had just begun the bed state, which didn't tally as usual, when the doors were opened once more, this time by a young man in a white hospital coat, his stethoscope crammed in its pocket. He looked tired and rather untidy, but neither of these things could dim his slightly arrogant good looks. He took a seat on the edge of the desk, right on top of the bed state, and said:

'Hullo, Phoebe—good lord, haven't you got any nurses about tonight? I've been hunting you all over. That coronary, he's gone up to Intensive Care, so that lightens your burden a bit, doesn't it?'

She smiled at him; she was a beautiful girl, and when she smiled she was quite dazzling. Before he had met her, he had always scoffed at descriptions of girls with sapphires in their eyes and corn-coloured hair, but he had been forced to admit that he was wrong, because Phoebe had both, with the added bonus of a small straight nose and a mouth which curved sweetly, and although she wasn't above middle height, her figure was good if a little on the plump side. She was, he had to own, quite perfect; the one small fact that she was twenty-seven, three years older than himself, he did his best to ignore; he would have preferred it otherwise, but one couldn't have everything. . . As soon as he had taken a couple more exams he would ask her to marry him. He hadn't intended to marry before he was thirty at least, with a fellowship and well up the ladder of success, but if he waited until then she would be thirty herself—a little old, although she would make a splendid wife for an ambitious young doctor, and looking at her now, she didn't look a day over twenty.

'Any chance of a cup of tea?' he wanted to know.

She didn't bother to tell him that she had missed her own midnight meal; that she would get a sketchy tea into the bargain. 'Yes—but you must be very quiet, I've only just got them all quiet again.' She got up. 'Keep an eye on the ward,' she begged, and slipped away to the kitchen.

She came back presently with two mugs, a thick slice of bread and butter atop each of them, and handed him his with a murmured: 'I haven't had my meal.'

'Poor old girl—I'll take you out for a good nosh on your nights off.'

'I can't, Jack, I'm going home. Sybil's got a week's holiday, and I haven't seen her for ages.'

Sybil was her younger sister, twenty-three and so like her that people who didn't know them well occasionally confused their identities, which was partly why Sybil, when she decided to be a nurse too, had gone to another training school—a London hospital and not very far away from St Gideon's—but what with studying for her finals and Phoebe being on night duty, they saw very little of each other. Soon it would be easier, Phoebe thought, taking a great bite out of her bread and butter, for Sybil had sat her hospital finals and the last of the State exams had been that morning. When she had qualified, as she would, for she was a clever girl, they would put their heads together and decide what they would do. The world, as the Principal Nursing Officer had told Phoebe when she had offered her the post of Night Sister, was her oyster. That had been three years ago and she still hadn't opened her particular oyster—there were jobs enough, but she had wanted to stay near Sybil until she was qualified. Now perhaps they would go abroad together.

Her train of thought was interrupted by her companion, who put down his mug, squeezed her hand and went out of the ward. Phoebe watched him go, the smile she had given him replaced by a tiny frown. He was going to ask her to marry him—she was aware of that and she didn't know what to do about it. She liked him very much, they got on well together—too well, she thought shrewdly—they had similar tastes and ideals, but surely, she asked herself for the hundredth time, there was more to it than that? And shouldn't she know if she loved him? Was this all that love was, a mild pleasure in someone's company, a sharing of tastes, a gentle acceptance of being a doctor's wife for the rest of her days—for Jack, she felt sure, would expect her to be just that and nothing more, she would never be allowed to steal the scene. Would her heart break if she never saw him again, or if, for that matter, he were to start taking some other girl out for a change? She was older than he; she had pointed this out to him on several occasions, and more than that, being a soft-hearted girl she had never allowed the thought that she found him very young upon occasion take root in her mind.

The hour ticked away. She solved the bed state, puzzled out the off duty for another two weeks, and was dealing with old Mrs Grey, who was a diabetic and showing all the signs and symptoms of a hyperglycaemic coma, when Nurse Small came back. They dealt with it together, then Phoebe, gathering up her papers and whispering instructions as to where she would be if she was wanted again, went silently from the ward, down the long corridor, chilly now in the small hours of an April morning, and into the office which was hers during the night when she had the time to sit in it. She had barely sat down when her bleep started up—Children's this time, and could she go at once because Baby Crocker had started a nasty laryngeal stridor. She had to get Jack up after a while; he came to the ward in slacks and a sweater over his pyjamas, and they worked on the child together, and when he finally went, half an hour later, she walked down the corridor with him, starting on her overdue rounds once more. At the end of the corridor, where he went through the door leading to the resident's quarters, he gave her a quick kiss, said 'See you' and disappeared, leaving her to make her way to Men's Medical on the ground floor, musing, as she went, on the fact that although his kiss had been pleasant, it hadn't thrilled her at all, and surely it should?

The early morning scurry gave her little time to think about herself. Fortified by a pot of strong tea, she did her morning rounds, giving a hand where it was wanted and then retiring to her office to write the report and presently to take it along to her daytime colleague before paying her final visit to the Night Super. A night like any other, she thought, yawning her way to breakfast, where Sadie Thorne, Night Sister on the Surgical side, was already waiting for her. Night Super was there too, a kindly, middle-aged woman,

whose nights were filled with paper work and
an occasional sortie into which ward was in difficulties. She was good at her job and well liked,
for she never failed to find help for a ward when
it was needed and had been known to roll up her
own sleeves and make beds when there was no
one else available. But normally, unless there
was dire emergency in some part of the hospital,
or a 'flu epidemic among the nurses, she did her
work unseen, supported by Phoebe and Sadie
and Joan Dawson, the Night Theatre Sister. She
looked up from her post now as Phoebe sat down,
wished her good morning just as though they
hadn't seen each other less than an hour since,
and went back to her letters, while Phoebe made
inroads on her breakfast, thinking contentedly
that in another twenty-four hours' time she
would be going home. She caught Sadie's eye
now and grinned at her.

'One more night,' she declared.

'Lucky you. Going home?'

Phoebe nodded. 'With Sybil—she's got a
week off and goes back to night duty.'

Night Super looked up briefly. 'I hear she did
very well in her hospitals.'

'Yes, Miss Dean. I don't know how well, but
I hope she's in the running for one of the prizes.'

'Like her sister,' murmured the Night Super,
and Phoebe, who had gained the gold medal of
her year, went a becoming pink.

She packed her overnight bag before she went
to bed, because on the following morning there
would be barely time for her to tear into her

clothes and catch the train. Then she washed her hair, and overcome by sleep, got into bed with it hanging like a damp golden curtain round her shoulders.

The night was fairly easy—the usual mild scares, the usual emergency admission, and hub-bub on the children's ward, because one of its small inmates was discovered to be covered in spots. Phoebe, called on the telephone by an urgent voice, made her way there as quickly as she could, sighing. It was early in the night, she still had her rounds to make.

The child was a new patient, admitted just as the day staff were handing over thankfully to their night colleagues, and not particularly ill. She was popped into a cot while the more urgent cases were attended to, presently she would be bathed, her hair washed, and tucked up for the night.

Phoebe, looking quite breathtakingly beauti-ful in her dark blue uniform, trod quietly down the ward with a nod to the nurses to get on with what they were doing and not mind her. The child was sitting on a blanket in its cot, eating a biscuit. It looked pale and undernourished and was, like so many of the children who were admitted, too small, too thin and lacklustre as to eye—not through lack of money, Phoebe knew, but through the parents' neglect; good-natured and unthinking, but still neglect. She smiled at the elderly little face, said brightly, 'Hullo, chick, what's your name?' and at the same time peered with an expert eye at the spots.

There were a great many of them, and when she peeped beneath the little flannel nightshirt there were a great many more. She straightened up and spoke to the nurse who had joined her. 'Fleas,' she said softly, so that no one would hear save her companion. 'Infected too. A mild Savlon bath, Nurse, usual hair treatment and keep a sharp eye open. Give her a milk drink and let me know if she doesn't settle. She's a bronchitis, isn't she? She'll be seen in the morning, but if you're worried let me know.' She turned away and then came back to say in a low voice: 'And wear a gown.' Her lovely eyes twinkled at the nurse, who smiled back. 'And I might as well do a round now I'm here, mightn't I?'

The night went smoothly after that. She was accustomed to, and indeed expected, the diabetic comas, coronaries and relapses which occurred during the course of it. She dealt with them as they arose with a calm patience and a sense of humour which endeared her to the rest of the night staff. She even had time for a quick cup of tea before she went to give her report.

She arrived at Waterloo with a couple of minutes to spare. There was no sign of Sybil— she would be on the train, a long train, and only its front carriages went to Salisbury; she jumped into the nearest door and started walking along the corridor. Her sister was in the front coach, sitting in an empty compartment with her feet comfortably on the seat opposite her, reading a glossy magazine. She was very like Phoebe, but her good looks were a little more vivid, her eyes a shade paler and her voice, when she spoke, just a tone higher.

'Hullo, Phoebe darling, here by the skin of your teeth, I see. How are you—it's ages since we saw each other.' She was putting Phoebe's bag on the rack as she spoke, now she pushed her gently into a window seat. 'Here, put your feet up and have a nap. We can talk later. I'll wake you in good time.'

And Phoebe, now that she had caught her train and greeted her sister, did just as Sybil suggested; in two minutes she was asleep. She wakened, much refreshed, at the touch on her arm and sat up, did her face, tidied her hair and drank the coffee Sybil had got for her, then said contritely: 'What a wretch I am—I quite forgot. How about the hospitals?'

Sybil grinned engagingly. 'The Gold Medal, ducky! I couldn't let you be the only one in the family with one, could I? I don't get the State results for six weeks, but I don't care whether I pass or not.' She looked secretive and mischievous at the same time, but when Phoebe said: 'Do tell—something exciting?' all she would say was: 'I'll tell you later, when there's no hurry. Look!'

The carriage door was flung open and a horde of people surged in, making conversation impossible. The train shuddered, gave a sigh as though it disliked the idea of leaving the station, and continued on its way. At Shaftesbury, they got out; they lived in a small village close to

Sturminster Newton, but Aunt Martha, who had moved in to look after them when their mother had died, and stayed on when their father died a few years later, liked to come and fetch them in the second-hand Austin which they had all three bought between them. She was on the platform now, in her tweed skirt and her twin-set, a felt hat of impeccable origin wedged on her almost black hair, only lightly streaked with grey despite her fifty-odd years. It framed her austere good looks and gave colour to her pale face, which broke into a smile as she saw them. She greeted them both with equal affection and walked them briskly to where the car was parked, telling Sybil to sit in front with her so that Phoebe, if she felt so inclined, could continue her nap undisturbed in the back.

Which she did without loss of time, waking after a blissful fifteen minutes to find that they were already going through East Orchard; at the next village, named, inevitably, West Orchard, they would turn off on to a side road which would bring them to Magdalen Provost, where they lived——a very small village indeed, which Phoebe had declared on several occasions to have more letters to its name than it had houses. It was a charming place, only a mile or so from the main road, and yet it had remained peacefully behind the times; even motor cars and the twice daily bus had failed to bring it up to date, and by some miracle it had remained undiscovered by weekend househunters looking for a holiday cottage, probably because it was so well hidden, awkward to get at, and in winter, impossible to get out of or into by car or bus because it lay snug between two hills rising steeply on either side, carrying a road whose gradient was more than enough for a would-be commuter.

Aunt Martha rattled down the hill and stopped in the centre of the village where the church, surrounded by a sprinkling of houses, the pub and the post office and village stores which were actually housed in old Mrs Deed's front room, stood. Phoebe's home stood a little apart from the rest, surrounded by a stone wall which enclosed a fair-sized, rather unkempt garden. The house itself wasn't large, but roomy enough, and she loved it dearly; she and Sybil had spent a happy childhood here with their parents, their father, a scientist of some repute, pursuing his engrossing occupation while their mother gardened and kept house and rode round the countryside on the rather fiery horse her husband had given her. Both girls rode too, but neither of them were with their mother when she was thrown and killed while they were still at school, and their father, considerably older than his wife, had died a few years later.

Aunt Martha drew up with a flourish before the door and they all went inside. It was a little shabby but not poorly so; the furniture was old and well cared for and even if the curtains and carpets were rather faded, there was some nice Georgian silver on the sideboard in the dining room. Phoebe, now wide awake, helped bring in the cases and then went upstairs to change into slacks and shirt before joining Aunt Martha in the kitchen for coffee, regaling that lady with the latest hospital news as they drank it, but when Sybil joined them, the talk, naturally enough, centred around her and her success. It wasn't for a few minutes that Phoebe came to the conclusion that it was she and their aunt who were excited about the results and not Sybil herself. She wondered uneasily why this was and whether it had something to do with whatever it was Sybil was going to tell her. Prompted by this thought, she asked:

'Shall we go for a walk after lunch, Syb?' and the uneasiness grew at the almost guilty look her sister gave her as she agreed.

They went to their favourite haunt—a copse well away from the road, with a clearing near its edge where a fallen tree caught the spring sun. They squatted comfortably on it and Phoebe said: 'Now, Sybil, let's have it. Is it something to do with St Elmer's or about your exams?'

Her sister didn't look at her. 'No—no, of course not—at least. . . Phoebe, I'm giving in my notice at the end of the week.'

Phoebe felt the uneasiness she had been trying to ignore stir, but all she said was: 'Why, love?'

'I'm going to get married.'

The uneasiness exploded like a bomb inside her. 'Yes, dear? Who to?'

'Nick Trent, he's the Medical Registrar. He's landed a marvellous job at that new hospital in Southampton. We're going to marry in two months' time—he gets a flat with the job and there's no reason for us to wait.'

'No, of course not, darling. What a wonderful surprise—I'm still getting over it.' Phoebe's voice was warm but bewildered. They had discussed the future quite often during the past six months or so and Sybil had never so much as hinted. . . They both went out a good deal, she had even mentioned Jack in a vague way, but she had always taken it for granted that the two of them would share a year together, perhaps in some post abroad. Sybil had known that, just as she had known that Phoebe had stayed at St Gideon's, waiting for her to finish her training. She asked in a voice which betrayed none of these thoughts: 'What's he like, your Nick?'

'I knew you'd be on my side, darling Phoebe.' Sybil told her at some length about Nick and added: 'He wanted to meet you and Aunt Martha. I thought we might fix a weekend—your next nights off, perhaps.'

'Yes, of course.'

'He's got a car——we could all come down together.'

Phoebe smiled. 'Nice—I shall be able to snore on the back seat,' and then, quietly: 'There's something else, isn't there, Syb?'

'Oh, Phoebe darling, yes, and I don't know what to do unless you'll help me. You see, a few weeks ago I was chosen to take a job in Holland. . .'

Phoebe had her head bowed over the tree-trunk, watching a spider at work. She said placidly: 'Yes, dear—go on.'

'Well, it's some scheme or other cooked up between St Elmer's and some hospital or other in Delft—there's a professor type who specialises in fibrocystitis—he's over here doing some research with old Professor Forbes, and the scheme is for a nurse from Delft to come over here and me to go there for two months. But first I'm supposed to go to the hospital where he's working—you know that children's hospital where they've got a special wing—the idea being that I shall be so used to his ways that it won't matter where I work. I thought it would be fun and I said I would, and then Nick...we want to get married.'

'Of course, but you could get married afterwards, dear. It would only be a few months—not long.'

Her young sister gave her a smouldering glance. 'Yes, it is,' she declared. 'I won't!'

'Well, tell your people at hospital that it's all off.'

'I can't—all the papers and things are signed and the hospital in Delft has made all the arrangements. Phoebe, will you go instead of me?'

'Will I *what*?' uttered Phoebe in a shocked voice.

'Go instead of me.'

'How can I possibly? It couldn't be done—it's absurd—they'd find out.'

'You know you're dying to leave and get off night duty and try something else for a change. Well, here's your chance.'

'But I'm not you.'

'Near enough, no one need know. No one's ever seen us at the children's hospital, nor in Delft, have they? Even if they had, we're so alike.'

'I thought you said the Dutch doctor had seen you?'

'Pooh, him--he looked half asleep; I don't think he even looked at me, and we were only together for a couple of minutes, and I hardly spoke.' She added persuasively: 'Do, darling Phoebe! It sounds mad, doesn't it? but no one's being harmed and it's not really so silly. And don't worry about the man, I doubt if he even noticed that I was a girl.' She sounded scornful.

'He sounds ghastly--I suppose he speaks English?'

'So well that you know he's not,' explained her sister, 'and he's got those vague good manners. . .'

'I'll not do it,' said Phoebe, and was horrified when Sybil burst into tears.

'Oh, dear,' she wailed through her sobs, 'now I don't know what I'll do--at least, I do. I shall run away and hide until Nick goes to Southampton and we'll get married in one of those pokey register offices and n-no one will come to the w-wedding!'

Phoebe sat watching her sister's lovely face. Even while she cried she was beautiful and very appealing and she loved her dearly--besides, she had promised her father that she would look after her. She said now: 'Don't cry, love--I'll do it. I think it's crazy and I'm not sure that if

I'm caught I shan't get sent to prison, but it's only for a couple of months and if you don't go someone else will, so it might as well be me. Only promise me that you'll have a proper wedding, the sort Mother and Father would have liked you to have. And are you sure about Nick? I mean really sure—it's for the rest of your life.'

Sybil smiled at her through her tears. 'Oh, Phoebe, I'm sure—I can't explain, but when you love someone like I love Nick, you'll know. You're a darling! We'll fix it all up while we're here, shall we? Just you and me—Nick doesn't know, I was so excited and happy I forgot to tell him and when I thought about it later I couldn't. And Aunt Martha. . .'

'We won't tell anyone at all,' said Phoebe. Now that she was resigned to the madcap scheme she found herself positively enjoying the prospect of a change of scene. 'I'm quite mad to do it, of course. Now begin at the beginning and tell me exactly what it's all about. Are you sure this doctor didn't get a good look at you?'

'Him? Lord, no, Phoebe. I told you, he's the sleepy kind, eyes half shut—I should think that half the time he forgets where he is. You'll be able to twist him round your little finger.'

'What's his name?'

Sybil looked vague. 'I can't remember. I'll find out for you, and the name of the hospital and where he lives and anything else I'm supposed to know.'

'Which reminds me—I don't know an awful

lot about fibrocystic disease—hasn't it got another name?'

'Mucoviscidosis, and you can forget it. The treatment hasn't changed much in the last year or so and you know quite enough about it—I remember telling me about several cases you had on the Children's Unit. . .'

'Three years ago,' murmured Phoebe.

'Yes, well. . .I'll bring you up to date, and what does it matter anyway, for the whole idea is that I—you should be seconded to this hospital so that you can learn all about this man's new ideas.'

'And afterwards? Am I supposed to go back to St Elmer's and spread the good news around?—then we are in the apple cart.'

'No, nothing like that. I'm free to do what I like when I come back from Holland. As far as St Elmer's goes, they think I'm giving in my notice so's I can get a job somewhere else when I get back to England.'

'My passport,' hazarded Phoebe suddenly. 'Supposing this man sees it? Or don't we travel together when we go?'

'Oh, yes, that's all been arranged, but remember the British and the non-British split up when they get to the Customs. Anyway, he's hardly likely to breathe over your shoulder, he's not that sort.'

'He sounds a dead bore,' Phoebe said slowly. 'I'm not sure. . .'

'You promised—besides, there are bound to be other people around—housemen and so forth.' She paused. 'I say, there's nothing serious between you and Jack, is there?'

Phoebe shook her head and said thoughtfully: 'And if there was, this is just what's needed to speed things up—I can't quite make up my mind...'

'Then don't,' said Sybil swiftly. 'Phoebe love, if it were the real thing, you wouldn't even stop to think—you'd know.' She grinned and got up. 'You see, this is just what you need, away from it all you'll have time to decide.'

Phoebe got to her feet. 'Perhaps you're right, love. Now tell me, you and your Nick, when do you want to get married?'

They spent the rest of their walk happily discussing wedding plans and clothes. Phoebe had a little money saved, but Sybil none at all.

'Well, that doesn't matter,' declared Phoebe. 'There's enough to buy you some decent clothes and pay for the wedding,' and when Sybil protested: 'I'm not likely to marry first, am I?' she wanted to know soberly, and then broke off to exclaim: 'Look—three magpies, they must have been eavesdropping. What is it now? One for anger, two for mirth, three for a wedding...'

They giggled happily and walked home arm-in-arm.

By the time Phoebe returned to St Gideon's from her nights off, she and Sybil had their plans laid, the first step of which was for her to resign immediately. It would work out very well, they had discovered; she would be due nights off before she left, time to go home, explain to Aunt Martha that she had taken a job with this Dutch doctor and would be going to Holland, collect the uniform Sybil's hospital were allowing her to keep until she returned to England, and make her way to the children's hospital, where, according to Sybil, she was expected. The one important point to remember was that for the time being, she was Sybil and not Phoebe.

She went to the office to resign on the morning after her return, to the utter amazement of the Chief Nursing Officer. She was a nice woman, interested in her staff and anxious to know what Phoebe intended to do—something, of course, which Phoebe was unable to tell her, for most of the big hospitals knew each other's business and probably the exchange scheme at St Elmer's was already common property. Miss Bates would hear sooner or later via the hospital grapevine, that Sybil had left to get married, probably she already knew that she had been seconded for the scheme, she wasn't above putting two and two together and making five.

'I haven't quite decided,' Phoebe told her, playing safe. 'I think I shall have a month or two's holiday at home.'

If Miss Bates considered this a curious statement from a member of her staff whom she knew for a fact depended upon her job for her bread and butter, she forbore from saying so. She thought Phoebe a nice girl, clever and remarkably beautiful. She hoped that she would marry, because she deserved something better than living out her life between hospital walls. Miss Bates was aware, just as the rest of the hospital, that the Medical Registrar fancied Night Sister Brook, but she was an astute woman, she thought that the affair was lukewarm and Sister Brook, despite her calm disposition, was not a lukewarm person. She sighed to herself, assured Phoebe that she would always be glad to see her back on the staff should she change her mind, and hoped that she would enjoy her holiday.

Phoebe didn't see Jack during her first night's duty; he had gone on a few days' leave and wouldn't be back for two more days—something for which she was thankful, for it seemed a good idea to let the hospital know that she was leaving first. The news would filter through to him when he got back and he would have time to get used to the idea before they encountered each other, as they were bound to do.

They met over the bed of a young girl three nights later—an overdose and ill; there was no time to say anything to each other, for the patient took all their attention, and when he left, almost an hour later, he gave her some instructions to pass on to the nurses, and walked away. Ten minutes later Phoebe left the ward herself. She had done her first round, thank heaven, so she could spare ten minutes for a cup of coffee. She opened the door of her office at the same time as the junior nurse on the ward arrived with the tray and she took it from her with a word of thanks, noting with a sinking heart that there were two cups on it—presumably Jack intended to have a cup with her. She pushed the door open and found him inside, standing by the desk, glowering.

He said at once; 'I'm told you're leaving. Rather sudden, isn't it?'

Phoebe sat down, poured coffee for them both and opened the biscuit tin before she answered him. 'Yes, Jack. I—I made up my mind while I was on nights off. Sybil's leaving too.'

He looked slightly mollified. 'Oh—you're off together somewhere, I suppose. For how long?'

'No—I've decided to have a little holiday, staying with relatives.' The idea had just that minute popped into her head and she hated lying to him, but after all, it wasn't his business. 'I feel unsettled.'

He stirred his coffee endlessly, looking at it intently. 'Yes, well, I suppose if you feel you must—I shall miss you, Phoebe, but I daresay you'll be ready to come back by the time I decide to marry. I shall ask you then.' He glanced up briefly. 'Everything has to be just as I want it first.'

That jarred. Was she not important enough to him—more important—than the set pattern he had laid out for them both, and without first finding out if she wanted it that way? She could see it all—the engagement when he was suitably qualified and had his feet on the first rung of the consultant's ladder, the wedding, the suitable home, suitably furnished, all the things that any girl would want, so why did she feel so rebellious?

It was all too tepid, she decided. It would be nice to be swept off her feet, to be so madly loved that the more mundane things of life didn't matter, to rush off to the nearest church without thought of the right sort of wedding. She passed him the sugar and sipped her coffee. If Nick could marry Sybil on his registrar's pay and find it wonderful, why couldn't Jack feel the same way? She began to understand a little of what Sybil had meant about loving someone, and she knew at that moment that she would never love Jack—like him, yes, even be fond of him, but that wasn't at all the same thing.

She said quietly: 'Jack, I can't stop you doing that, but I don't think it's going to be any use.' She stared at him over the rim of her mug, her lovely eyes troubled.

'I'll be the best judge of that,' he told her a shade pompously, 'and until then I prefer not to discuss it.'

He was as good as his word; they discussed the patient they had just left until, with a huffy good night, he went away.

She should mind, Phoebe told herself when she was alone. She had closed the door on a settled future, and just for a moment she was a little scared; she was twenty-seven, not very young any more, and although she could have married half a dozen times in the last few years, that was of no consolation to her now. She sighed and pulled the bed state towards her. It seemed likely that she was going to be an old maid.

# CHAPTER TWO

A MONTH later, on her way to Magdalen Pròvost, St Gideon's behind her, the doubtful future before her, Phoebe reflected that everything had gone very well—there had been no snags, no one had wanted to know anything, no awkward questions had been asked. Sybil had already left and was at home making plans for her wedding to Nick, whom Phoebe considered to be all that could be desired as a brother-in-law. Sybil was going to be happy; now that she had met him Phoebe had to admit that in Sybil's place, she would have done exactly as she had done. Even Aunt Martha had accepted everything calmly— she had liked Nick too, had been generous in her offers of help to the bride, and was entering into the pleasurable excitement of a wedding in the family with a great deal more zest than Phoebe had supposed she would. And as for her own future, when she had told her aunt what she intended doing, without bringing Sybil's part into it at all, the older lady had wholly endorsed her plans.

'It's high time you had a change,' she stated approvingly, 'it sounds a most interesting scheme and you'll enjoy a change of scene. What did Jack have to say?'

Phoebe had told her rather worriedly and

added: 'I feel guilty, Aunt, but honestly, I didn't let him think that I. . .I don't think I encouraged him at all; we just sort of liked being together.'

'Well, my dear,' her aunt had said briskly, 'there's a good deal more to being in love than liking each other's company, and I'm sure you know that. Have you been able to convince him, or does he still think you might change your mind?'

'I told him I wouldn't do that.'

She remembered the conversation now, sitting in the train, and wondered what would happen if she suddenly discovered that she had made a mistake and was in love with Jack after all, and then dismissed the idea because they had known each other for a year or more and surely by now she would have some other feeling for him other than one of friendship. She decided not to think about it any more—not, in fact, to think of anything very deeply, but to take each day as it came, at least until she returned to England.

It was Nick and Sybil who met her at Shaftesbury, for Nick was spending a day or so at Magdalen Provost before taking Sybil to meet his parents. They discussed the wedding as he drove his car, a Saab, rather too fast but very skilfully, in the direction of the village, but presently he interrupted to ask: 'Phoebe, what's the name of this man you're going to work for? I've an idea I know something about him.'

'Oh, good,' said Phoebe lightly, 'because I don't—his name's van Someren.'

Nick tore past an articulated wagon at a speed

which made her wince. 'I knew his name rang
a bell,' her future relative told her cheerfully.
'Old van Someren—met him at one of those
get-togethers. . .'

'Then you can tell me something about him,'
said Phoebe firmly.

'Don't know anything—surely your people
have given you all the gen?'

'Oh, I don't mean that. How old is he, and is
he nice, and is he married?'

They were going down the hill into the village
at a speed which could if necessary, take them
through it and up the other side. 'Good lord, I
don't know—thirty, forty, I suppose—and what
do you mean by nice? To look at, his morals,
his work?'

'Just. . .oh, never mind, you tiresome thing.
You're not much help. There's ten years between
thirty and forty, but perhaps you haven't
noticed.'

Nick laughed and brought the car to a sudden
halt outside the house. 'Poor Phoebe—I'd have
taken a photo of him if I'd known. Tell you one
thing, though, I'm sure someone told me that
he's got a boy, so he must be married.' He turned
in his seat to look at her. 'When do you go,
tomorrow?'

'On an afternoon train. I said I'd arrive at the
hospital in the evening.'

'We'll take you in to Shaftesbury—we'd go
the whole way, but we've still got to see the
parson about this and that.' They were all out of
the car by now, loitering towards the door.

'You'll be at the wedding, won't you?'

It was Sybil who answered for her. 'Of course she will. I know I'm not having any bridesmaids, but Phoebe's going to be there,' she turned to her sister, 'and you'd better be in something eye-catching, darling.'

'It's your day, Syb. I thought of wearing dove grey—that's if Doctor van Someren allows me to come.'

'You'll have days off—all you have to do is save them up and tell him you have to attend a wedding. Anyway, didn't I read somewhere that the Dutch set great store on family gatherings? Of course you'll be able to come.'

She sounded so worried that Phoebe said reassuringly: 'Don't you worry, I wouldn't miss it for the world.'

They went indoors then, to Aunt Martha, busy in a kitchen which smelled deliciously of something roasting in the oven, and no one mentioned the Dutch doctor again.

Twenty-four hours never went so quickly. Phoebe, joining the queue at Waterloo station for a taxi, felt as though she hadn't been home at all. She would miss going down to Magdalen Provost and she doubted very much if she would get another opportunity of a weekend before she left England. She had quite forgotten to ask Sybil the arrangements for her off-duty, but surely she would manage a day or two before she left the children's hospital. She got out of the taxi, paid the man and rang the visitors bell of the Nurses' Home. If anyone wanted to see her so late in the day, the warden would doubtless give her the message. But there was only a request that she should present herself at the Principal Officer's office at nine o'clock the next morning, and when she stated simply that she was Nurse Brook, the warden hadn't wanted to know any more than that, but took her up to a rather pleasant little room, offered her a warm drink and wished her good night. So far, so good, Phoebe told her reflection in the mirror, and went to bed and slept soundly.

The Principal Nursing Officer was brisk and busy. As Phoebe went into the room she said: 'Ah, yes, Nurse Brook. Splendid. Will you go along to the Children's Unit and they'll put you in the picture—I'm sure it has already been made clear to you that this scheme is housed here temporarily, and it's run quite separately from the hospital itself. Anything you want to know, there will be someone you can ask there.'

She smiled quite kindly in dismissal and pulled a pile of papers towards her, and Phoebe, murmuring suitably, got herself out of the office, sighing with relief that it had all been so easy, aware at the same time that she should be feeling guilty and failing to do so because she remembered Sybil's happy face.

The Children's Unit was across the yard. Supposedly there was another way to it under cover, but she couldn't see it and it was a lovely sunny day and she welcomed the chance to be out of doors, if only for a minute or two. The door stood open on to the usual tiled, austere entrance, a staircase ascending from it on one side, a row of doors lining its other wall. On the one marked 'Doctor van Someren' she knocked, for it seemed good sense to get to the heart of the matter at once. No one answered, so she opened the door and went inside. It was a small room and rather dreary, with a large desk with its swivel chair, shelves full of books and papers and two more chairs, hard and uncomfortable, ranged against one wall. Phoebe, who had seen many such offices, wasn't unduly depressed at this unwelcoming scene, however. Hospitals, she had learned over the years, were not run for the comfort of their staff. There was an inner door, too. She crossed the room and tapped on it and a woman's voice said 'Come in.' It was an exact copy of the room she had just left, only smaller, and had the additions of a typewriter and a woman using it. She wasn't young any more and rather plain, but she looked nice and when Phoebe said: 'I'm Nurse Brook and I'm not at all sure where I'm supposed to be,' she smiled in a friendly fashion.

'Here,' she answered cheerfully, 'if you like to go back to the other room, I'll see if Doctor van Someren is available. I expect you want to start work at once.'

She went back with Phoebe to the doctor's room, waved a hand at one of the chairs and disappeared. Phoebe sat for perhaps ten seconds, but it was far too splendid a day not to go to the window and look out. It was too high for her to see much; obviously whoever had built the place

had considered it unnecessary for the occupants
to refresh themselves with a glimpse of the outside world. But by standing on tiptoe she was
able to see quite a pretty garden, so unexpected
that she opened the bottom sash in order to examine it with greater ease.

She didn't hear the door open. When she
turned round at last, she had no idea how long
the man had been standing there. She frowned a
little and went a faint pink because it was hardly
the way she would want an interview to begin,
with her leaning out of the window, showing a
great deal more leg than she considered dignified
for a Ward Sister—but then she wasn't a Ward
Sister—she really would have to remember. . .
And he wasn't in the least like the picture Sybil
had painted of him. He was a big, broad-
shouldered man and very tall, something her
sister had forgotten to mention, and she, for that
matter, had forgotten to ask. His hair was the
colour of straw which she thought could be
streaked with grey; it was impossible to tell until
she got really close to him. And she was deeply
astonished to find him good-looking in a beaky-
nosed fashion, with a firm mouth which looked
anything but dreamy, and there was nothing
vague about the piercing blue gaze bent upon
her at the moment.

'Miss Brook,' his voice was deep, 'Miss
Sybil Brook?'

She advanced from the window. 'Yes, I'm
Miss Brook,' she informed him pleasantly,
pleased that she didn't have to tell a downright

fib so soon in the conversation. There would be time enough for that; she only hoped that she wouldn't get confused. . . 'You're Doctor van Someren, I expect. How do you do?' She held out her small capable hand and had it gripped in a gentle vice. For one startled moment she wondered if he could be the same man whom Sybil had seen, and then knew that it was; his face had become placid, his eyelids drooping over eyes which seemed half asleep, his whole manner vague.

'Er—yes, how do you do?' He smiled at her. 'I think it would be best if I were to take you to the ward—you can talk to Sister Jones, and later there will be some notes and so on which I should like you to study.' He went over to the desk and picked up a small notebook and put it in his pocket, saying as he did so: 'I'm sometimes a little absentminded. . . I shall be doing a ward round in an hour, I should like you to be there, please.'

He sat down at the desk and began to open a pile of letters stacked tidily before him, quite absorbed in the task, so that after a few minutes Phoebe ventured to ask: 'Shall I go to the ward now, sir?'

He looked up and studied her carefully, just as though he had never set eyes on her before. 'Ah—Miss Brook, Miss Sybil Brook,' he reminded himself. 'I really do apologise. We'll go at once.'

Following him out of the room and up the stairs Phoebe could understand why Sybil had

described him as vague—all to the good; she
saw little reason for him to discover that she
wasn't Sybil; she doubted if he had really looked
at her, not after that first disconcerting stare.

Sister Jones was expecting her, and to
Phoebe's relief turned out to be a girl of about
her own age, with a cheerful grin and soft Welsh
voice which had a tendency to stammer. She
greeted the doctor with a friendly respect and
Phoebe was a little surprised to hear him address
her as Lottie. She hoped he wasn't in the habit
of addressing his nursing staff by their christian
names, for not only would she find it difficult to
answer to Sybil, she discovered at that moment
that she had no wish to tell him a fib. He was
too nice—an opinion presently endorsed when
he did his ward round; he was kind too and his
little patients adored him.

There were ten children in the ward, most of
them up and about, full of life and filled, too,
with a capacity for enjoyment which fibrocystics
seemed to possess as a kind of bonus over and
above a child's normal capacity to enjoy itself.
They were bright too, with an intelligence
beyond their years, as though they were being
allowed to crowd as much as possible into a life
which would possibly be shortened. The small
boy Doctor van Someren was examining at that
moment was thin and pale, but he laughed a good
deal at the doctor's little jokes, discussed the
cricket scores and wanted to know who Phoebe
was. The doctor told him briefly and went

on: 'And now, how about that tipping and tapping, Peter?'

A question which called forth a good deal of sheepish glances and mutterings on Peter's part. He didn't like hanging over his bed, being thumped by a nurse at six o'clock in the morning, he said so now with considerable vigour, and everyone laughed, but instead of leaving it at that, Phoebe was glad to see the doctor sit down on the side of the bed once more and patiently explain just why it was good for Peter to hang head downwards the minute he woke up each morning. Having made his point Doctor van Someren strolled towards the next bed, murmuring as he went:

'What a sad thing it is that this illness is so difficult to tackle.' He looked at Phoebe as he spoke and seemed to expect an answer, so she said: 'Yes, it is, but I'm afraid I don't know enough about it to pass any opinion.'

'A refreshing observation,' he said surprisingly. 'I find, during the course of my work, that there are a distressing number of people who have a great deal too much opinion and very little sense. I fancy that you have plenty of sense, Nurse Brook.' He nodded at her in a kindly way, sat down on the next bed and became instantly absorbed in its occupant. Phoebe, standing close behind him, found herself wondering how old he was. She had been right, there was quite a lot of grey mixed in with the straw-coloured hair. She guessed forty, but a moment later when he turned his head to speak to Sister Jones, and she could study his face, she decided that he was a good deal younger than that.

She had been a little disturbed to find that she was to go to Delft in ten days' time, for she had imagined that it would be longer than that, as it wasn't very long in which to get to know the doctor and his methods, and now she very much doubted if she would be able to get home again before she went, for Sister Jones had explained at some length that it was hoped that she would take her days off singly because the time was too short for her to miss even two days together; there was so much for her to learn. She had agreed because there was nothing else she could do, and in any case she would be going home for the wedding——she dragged her thoughts away from that interesting topic and applied herself to what the doctor was saying. He had some interesting theories and a compelling way of talking about them which held one's attention; by the end of the day she found herself deeply interested, both in the man and his ideas, and was a little surprised to find that the ward seemed very empty without him, rather like a room without its furniture, and yet he was a quiet man, there was nothing flamboyant about him—— indeed, when he wasn't actually engaged in his work, he was positively retiring.

In her room, after a friendly cup of tea with the other staff nurses, Phoebe undressed slowly, thinking about him, and when she was finally ready for bed she didn't go to sleep immediately, but sat up against the pillows, her golden hair cascading round her shoulders, her lovely face, devoid of the small amount of make-up she used, creased in a thoughtful frown. It wasn't turning out a bit as she had expected—she had expected to feel regrets, even guilt, but she didn't feel either, only a faint excitement and a certainty that she was going to enjoy every minute of Sybil's scheme.

Her feelings were strengthened during the next ten days; it seemed strange to be a staff nurse again, but Sister Jones was a dear and the other nurses were pleasant to work with. There was plenty of work on the ward, for Doctor van Someren was a man who expected his orders to be carried out to the letter, and it was sometimes hard and exacting. He had given Phoebe a number of books to read, some of them written by himself, and she couldn't help but be impressed by the string of letters after his name. He was undoubtedly clever, which might account for his moments of vagueness and for his habit of staring at her, which at first she had found a little trying until she decided that he was probably deep in thought and wasn't even aware of her.

She was to spend five nights on duty, because there was a good deal to do at night and he wanted her to be conversant with that as well, and to her surprise Doctor van Someren had himself suggested that she should have two days off afterwards so that she could go home before returning to London to meet him for the journey. He had offered no information about the trip.

She supposed they would travel by train and cross from Harwich, and although she would have liked to know very much, she hadn't liked to ask him because he had appeared so preoccupied when he had told her; he had moved away even as he was speaking, his registrar and housemen circling around him like satellites round their sun.

Phoebe hadn't been best pleased about going on nights, although she didn't care to admit to herself that the main reason for this was because she wouldn't see Doctor van Someren—and she liked seeing him, even though he was a married man and never seemed to see her at all. Apparently he had no eyes for women, however lovely—unlike his Registrar and George the houseman, both of whom found her company very much to their liking. She sighed and wondered, not for the first time, what his wife was like, then pushed the ward doors open, ready to take the day report from Sister Jones on her first night on. Life seemed strangely-dissatisfying.

The children took a lot of settling; she and Rawlings, the student nurse on with her, were still hard at it when Doctor van Someren came quietly into the ward. Phoebe laid the little girl carefully on to the pillows stacked behind her, conscious that her heart was beating a good deal faster than it should do.

'Any trouble?' he asked quietly, and she shook her head and smiled at him because it was so nice to see him unexpectedly.

'No, thank you, sir. They're very good, but

we've still got two more to see to.' She was apologetic because it was almost nine o'clock, but he made no sign of having heard her, only stood looking down on the child, comfortable and sleepy now, and presently he went away.

He came each night, conveying without words that his visits were simply because he liked the children and not because he had doubts as to his nurses' ability. And in the small hours of the night—her third night on, when Andrew, the ten-year-old in the corner bed, died, he was there again, with his registrar and Night Sister. But Phoebe noticed none of them, doing what she had to do with a heavy heart, and later, when there was no more to be done, going into the kitchen on some excuse or other because if she didn't shed some of the tears her throat would burst. She neither saw nor heard Doctor van Someren; it was his apologetic little cough which caused her to spin round to face him. She said wildly: 'You see, I'll be no good for your scheme—I can't bear it when this happens—he was so little.'

She wiped the back of her hand across her eyes to blot the tears, and despite them, her lovely face was quite undimmed.

The doctor said nothing for a moment, but crossed to the table, ladled tea into the pot, lifted the boiling water from the gas ring and made the tea. 'On the contrary, you will be very good, because you feel deeply about it.' He looked at her and in a voice suddenly harsh, asked: 'And how do you suppose I feel?'

She sniffled, 'Awful. I'm sorry.' She began to gather mugs on to a tray. 'I mean I'm sorry because I'm being a fool, and I'm sorry for you too, because this happens despite all you do.'

He took the tray from her. 'You are kind, Miss Brook, but the boot is on the other foot—soon we shall win our battle, you know.' He kicked open the door. 'And now dry your eyes and have a cup of your English tea—I should warn you that in Holland our tea is not as you make it, but our coffee is genuine coffee, which is more than I can say for the abomination I am offered here.' He smiled at her and she found herself smiling back at him; he really was nice—absentminded, perhaps, a little pedantic and, she fancied, old-fashioned in his views, but definitely nice.

But the sadder side of her work was seldom in the ascendant—there was a good deal of fun with the children too, and the nurses, under Sister Jones' rules, were a happy crowd. And over and above that, Doctor van Someren's enthusiasm spilled itself over the lot of them, so that very soon Phoebe found herself looking forward to going to Holland, where, so Sister Jones told her, his work was having a steady success—no spectacular results, just a slow, sure improvement in his little patients. She found herself wishing that she, in her small way, would be able to help him to attain his goal.

There was a party on the ward—a farewell party for Doctor van Someren—on her last night on duty. She got up an hour or so earlier than usual and went along to help with the peeling of oranges, the dishing out of ice-cream and the wiping of sticky hands. It was noisy and cheerful and it would have been even greater fun if various important people to do with the hospital hadn't been there too, to take up the guest of honour's time and attention. All the same, he found the time to wish each child goodbye and then crossed the ward to thank Phoebe for her help and to hope that the children would settle.

'They will give you a little trouble, perhaps,' he hazarded, 'and strictly speaking it is not good for them, but they must have their fun, don't you agree, Miss Brook?'

She nodded understandingly, aware as he was that during the early part of the night there would be a great deal of chatter and requests for drinks of water, and little tempers as well as tears, but they would sleep eventually and they had loved every minute of it. She looked around her, reflecting how strange it was that a few paper hats and balloons could create a party for a child.

He turned away. 'I shall see you here at seven o'clock in the evening, on the day after tomorrow,' he reminded her, and before she could ask how they were to go to Holland, he had gone, large and quiet, and very quickly.

She spent two busy days at home; there was a great deal she would have liked to discuss with Sybil, but somehow Aunt Martha always seemed to be with them, and beyond a few safe commonplaces about her work, she could say very little. Only when they had gone to bed, Sybil had come along to her room and sat on the bed and demanded to know if everything was all right.

Phoebe nodded. 'I think so—you were quite right, Doctor van Someren is absentminded, but only sometimes. He's a splendid doctor though. I expected him to be older—he seems older than he really is, I think, but only when he's worried. I like the work. . .'

Sybil interrupted her happily. 'There, didn't I say that it was a good thing when you agreed to go instead of me? And I bet you're far better at it than I should ever be. How are you going to Holland?'

'I don't know—I've been told to go to the hospital tomorrow evening at seven o'clock, that's all. What clothes shall I take?'

It was well after midnight before this knotty problem was solved to their entire satisfaction. Phoebe, remembering the doctor's gentle remark that he hoped that she wouldn't have too much luggage, decided to take one case, a small overnight bag and her handbag—a stout leather one capable of holding everything she was likely to need en route. The overnight bag she stuffed with night things, and as many undies as she could cram into it, and the case she packed under Sybil's critical eye with uncrushable cotton dresses, sandals, two colourful swimsuits, a sleeveless jersey dress in a pleasing shade of blue, a very simple dress in strawberry pink silk and, as a concession to a kindly fate, a pastel patterned party dress which could be rolled into a ball if necessary and still look perfection itself.

This task done, she felt free to wish her sister good night and go to bed herself. Not that she slept for several hours; her mind was too full of her job, and woven in and out of her more prosaic thoughts was the ever-recurring reflection that she was pleased that she would be seeing a good deal more of Doctor van Someren during the next few weeks.

The morning was taken up with last-minute chores and a discussion about the wedding, coupled with a strong reminder from Aunt Martha to make very sure that she returned home for it. She was thinking how best to settle this matter when her taxi drew up outside the hospital entrance and she stepped out. There was no one about. Through the glass doors she could see the head porter's back as he trod ponderously in the direction of the covered way at the back of the hall—perhaps she should go after him and find out. . . She actually had her hand on the door when Doctor van Someren said from behind her:

'Good evening, Miss Brook. You are rested, I hope? If you would come with me?'

It annoyed her that she felt flustered. She wished him a good evening in her turn in a rather cool voice and followed him to the hospital car park.

They stopped beside a claret-coloured Jaguar XJ12 and she tried to conceal her surprise, but her tongue was too quick for her. 'My goodness,' she exclaimed, 'is this yours?'

He looked faintly surprised. 'Yes—you didn't

tell me that you disliked travelling by car. It is the simplest way. . .'

'Oh, I don't—I love it. Only she's so splendid and she took my breath—I didn't expect. . . And I'm sure it's the simplest way, only I don't know which way that is.'

He put down her case and bag the better to give her his full attention. 'Did I not tell you how we should be travelling?'

She shook her head.

'Dear me—you must forgive me. By car, of course. We shall load it on to the Harwich boat and drive to Delft from the Hoek when we land in the morning. You are a good sailor?'

'Yes—though I've only crossed to Calais twice. We nearly always went by plane, and I loathed it.'

'We?' he prompted her gently.

'My mother and father and s. . .' she stopped just in time, 'me,' she added lamely, and felt her cheeks warm, but he didn't seem to notice and she drew a relieved breath. How fortunate it was that he wasn't an observant man, only with his patients. He picked up her case and put it in the boot, already packed with books and cases and boxes—no wonder he had hoped that she wouldn't bring too much luggage with her.

It was extraordinary how many times during their journey to Harwich that she had to stop to think before she replied to his casual questions. She hadn't realised before how often one mentioned one's family during the course of even the most ordinary conversation; she seemed to be continually fobbing him off with questions of her own about his work, their journey, details of the hospital where she would be working—anything, in fact, but her own home life. It was a relief when he slid the car to a halt in the Customs shed, a relief tempered with regret, though, because he was a most agreeable companion and she had found herself wishing that she could have told him all about Sybil and Nick, and her own part in the deception they were playing upon him. When she had consented to take Sybil's place she hadn't thought much about the other people involved; now she found that it mattered quite a lot to her.

They had a meal on board and Phoebe talked feverishly about a dozen subjects, taking care not to mention her home or her family, and the doctor made polite comments upon her sometimes rather wild statements, and didn't appear to be aware of the fact that she repeated herself upon occasion, but as soon as they had had their coffee, he observed pleasantly: 'I expect you would like to go to your cabin, Miss Brook,' and stood up as he said it, so that there was nothing else for her to do. Besides, he had a briefcase with him; he was already opening it when she looked back on her way out of the restaurant.

Possibly, she thought crossly, he had been dying for her to go for hours past. She undressed slowly and hung her oatmeal-coloured dress and jacket carefully away so that they would be creaseless and fresh in the morning. 'Not that it would matter,' she told herself, getting crosser.

'If I wore hot pants and a see-through blouse he wouldn't notice!'

She lay down on her bunk, determined not to go to sleep so that she would be able to tell him that she had spent an uncomfortable night—no, not uncomfortable, she corrected herself—it was a delightful cabin, far more luxurious than she had expected, certainly first class and on the promenade deck. It surprised her that the hospital authorities were willing to spend so much money on a nurse. She would have been just as comfortable sharing a cabin with another girl, although she doubted if she would have had the cheerful services of the stewardess who promised tea at six o'clock and begged her to ring her bell should she require anything further. With difficulty Phoebe brought her sleepy mind back to Doctor van Someren; it would be nice if she were to see a great deal of him in hospital—presumably she would be working on one of his wards, but perhaps he would leave the actual instruction to one of the more junior members of his team. She frowned at the idea and went to sleep.

She slept all night and, much refreshed by her tea, dressed, did her face and hair with care and went along to join the doctor for breakfast, looking as though she had slept the clock round and spent several leisurely hours over her toilette. His eyes, very bright beneath the arched colourless brows, swept over her and then blinked lazily. He wished her a good morning, hoped she had slept well and begged her to sit down to breakfast, something she was only too glad to do. Coffee and toast would be delightful, but the ship seemed to be a hive of activity and they had already docked; perhaps he hadn't noticed. She mentioned it diffidently, to be instantly reassured by his easy: 'I have a theory that it is quicker to be last off the ship.' A remark which, it turned out, was perfectly true, for by the time they had finished, the last of the passengers were leaving the ship and the Jaguar was swinging in mid-air, on its way to dry land.

There was no delay in the Customs shed but a good deal of talk in Dutch, which sounded like so much nonsense in her ears, so that she didn't pay attention but stood looking about her. She was recalled from this absorbing pastime by Doctor van Someren's voice and she turned at once to answer him and in the same split second was aware that he had called her Phoebe and she had responded. She felt the colour leave her face and then flood back, washing her from neck to forehead with a delicate pink. She would have liked to have said something—anything, but her brain, like her tongue, was frozen. It was the doctor who spoke.

'Very interesting. I have been wanting to do that since we met.' His voice was thoughtful, but she could have sworn that he was secretly amused. He turned away to speak to a porter and she followed him to where the car stood waiting in the cobbled yard beyond the station. It was only after she had got into it and he had taken the seat beside her that she asked in a small voice: 'How did you know my name?' and then:

'Are you going to send me back?'

He didn't look at her. 'Your sister mentioned you, and no—why should I? You are an admirable nurse, obviously far more experienced than you wished me to believe. I don't know the reason for the deception, but I imagine it was a sufficiently good one.'

'When did you find out?'

He sounded surprised. 'When we met, naturally.'

She faltered a little. 'But Sybil and I are so alike, people can never tell us apart, only when we're together, or—or they look at us properly.'

'And your sister decided that I hadn't studied her for a sufficient length of time to make your substitution risky. You are not in the least like her.'

They were already out of the town, tearing along the highway, but she really hadn't noticed that. She opened her mouth to refute this opinion, but he went on smoothly: 'No, don't argue, Miss Phoebe Brook. I'm not prepared to enlarge upon that at the moment, you will have to take my word for it.'

Phoebe stared out at the flat countryside without seeing any of it.

'I'm very sorry,' she told him stiffly, and thought how inadequate it was to say that. She was sorry and ashamed and furious with herself for playing a trick on him. 'It was a rotten thing to do. At the time, when Sybil—when I arranged to do it, it seemed OK I hadn't met you then,' she added naïvely, and failed to see his slow smile and the gleam in his eyes.

He gave the Jag her head. 'Do you care to tell me about it? But only if you wish. . .'

She felt quite sick. 'It's the least I can do.' She stared miserably at a group of black and white cows bunched round a man in the middle of a field as green and flat as a billiard table. 'I'm the one to blame,' she began, faintly aggressive in case he should argue the point, and when he didn't: 'You see, Sybil wants to get married—quite soon. . .' She was reminded of something. 'I should like to save up my days off and go home for the wedding, though I don't suppose you have anything to do with the nurses' off duty.'

They were in the heavy early morning traffic now and approaching a town. 'Is that Delft?' she wanted to know.

'Yes, it is. I have nothing to do with the nurses' off duty,' he was laughing silently again and she frowned, 'but I imagine I might be able to bring my influence to bear.'

To her surprise he edged the car into the slow lane and then into the lay-by ahead of them, switched off the engine and turned to look at her intently. 'Perhaps if I were to ask you a few questions it would be easier for both of us.' He didn't wait for her to answer him. 'Supposing you tell me where you were working to begin with. You are older than your sister,' he shot her a hooded glance, 'and I think that you have held a more responsible post. . .'

She choked on pricked vanity—did she look

such an old hag, then? Very much on her dignity, she said stiffly: 'I was Night Sister at St Gideon's—the medical block. I'm twenty-seven, since you make such a point of it. . .' She paused because he had made a sound suspiciously like a chuckle. 'I will explain exactly what happened. . .'

She did so, concisely and with a brevity which did justice to her years of giving accurate reports without loss of time. When she had finished she stole a look at him, but he was staring ahead, his profile, with its forceful nose and solid chin, looked stern. Perhaps he was going to send her back after all. She conceded that she deserved it. But all he said in a mild voice was: 'Good, that's cleared the air, then,' started the car again and allowed it to purr back into the stream of fast-moving traffic. 'The hospital is in the heart of the city. It's not new—there is a very splendid one, you must go over it while you are here — but the one in which you will work is very old indeed and although we have everything we require, it is dark and awkward. But the children are happy and that is the main thing. You will be on a sixteen-bedded ward of fibrocystics, but all the research work is done at the new hospital—St Jacobus.'

She found her voice. 'What's the hospital called—the one where I shall be?'

'St Bonifacius. You'll find that most of the staff speak English, and as for the children, I have discovered long ago that they will respond to any language provided it is spoken in the right tone of voice. Besides, there are a number of words which are so similar in both languages that I have no doubt you will get by.'

She hoped it would be as easy as it sounded. They were going slowly now through the compact little city, its winding streets lined with old houses, some of them so narrow that there was only room for a front door and a window, some so broad and solid that they should have been surrounded by parklands of their own. The streets were intersected by canals linked by narrow white bridges. She had the impression that she would be lost immediately she set foot outside the hospital door.

The silence had lasted a long time. Phoebe asked in a polite voice:

'Is the hospital a medical school? Were you a student here?'

'No—at Leyden, a few miles away, but my home is in Delft—has been for very many years. I took over the practice from my father. Now I devote almost all my time to fibrocystics.'

He turned the car into a narrow cobbled street where there were no pavements and barely room for the car. 'A short cut,' he explained, 'but when you go walking, I advise you to keep to the main streets until you know your way around.'

Nothing was further from her intention than to go roaming off with nothing but a foreign tongue in her head and a poor sense of direction, but there seemed no point in mentioning it to him. She said like an obedient child: 'No, I won't, sir,' and remained silent while he eased the Jaguar through high gates leading to a paved courtyard where several cars were parked and an ambulance was discharging its patient through a heavy door strong enough to have withstood a siege.

Her companion came to a gentle and accurate halt between the ambulance and a large Citroën, and got out. He had her door open before she could reach for it, saying easily: 'Your luggage will be seen to,' and led her briskly through the hospital entrance, where he spoke to the porter before turning to her and saying: 'I hope you will be happy while you are here with us.'

His tone was formal enough, but his smile was so kind that she found herself saying: 'I'm so sorry—the only way I can make you believe that is by working hard, and I promise you I will.'

He took her hand. 'I know you will, and if it is any comfort to you, Phoebe, I am not sorry and I can see no reason for you to be, either.'

She stared up into his face. Such a kind man, she thought confusedly, and perhaps people took advantage of his kindness—she hoped his wife looked after him. He didn't let go of her hand, and when she heard footsteps advancing towards them from the back of the square hall, she was glad of its firm reassuring grip. The footsteps belonged to a rather dumpy little woman in a dark grey uniform with a prim white collar.

The doctor held out his other hand, saying pleasantly in English.

'Directrice, how nice to see you again—here is our English nurse, Miss Brook. I leave her in your capable hands.' He smiled a little vaguely at them, murmured goodbye and went out of the door again, and Phoebe, still feeling his hand on hers, smiled uncertainly at the little lady before her.

# CHAPTER THREE

THE rest of the day was exciting, tiring and somewhat frustrating; everything was just a little different. She had accompanied the Directrice to her office, drunk coffee and listened to the details of the life she would lead while she was in the hospital, given in a fluent though sometimes quaint English; her salary, her off duty—which the Ward Sister would discuss with her—the length of hours she would work, the advisability of getting herself a dictionary at the first convenient moment. . . Full of undigested information, she was handed over to the Nurses' Home warden, a white-overalled, elderly woman who walked her through a great many corridors and small passages, an odd staircase or two and through a door in a wall which opened into a modern hallway. That at least, thought Phoebe, was exactly the same as the hall in the Nurses' Home at St Gideon's. Apparently hospital decorators the world over had the same unimaginative ideas about dark varnished wood and pale green walls. But her room, when she reached it, was pleasant, with a gay bedspread and curtains and a cheerful rug. Left to herself, she unpacked, changed into her uniform and mindful of her instructions, found her way back to the hospital and into Zaal Drie.

Zaal Drie was really three smallish wards, connected to each other by means of archways driven into the ancient walls of the hospital, the only evidence of the building's great age, for the beds, furniture and furnishings were modern and brightly coloured. There were flowers too and some budgerigars adding their tiny voices to the cheerful din, for it was already mid-morning and those children who were up were having lessons at a centre table in the first ward. They paused in whatever it was they were reciting under the direction of their young teacher and turned to stare at Phoebe, who stared back, wondering what she should do next—a problem solved for her; a small door beside her opened and the Ward Sister came out.

Doctor van Someren had told her that everyone would speak English, but she hadn't expected quite the degree of fluency she was encountering. Zuster Witsma addressed her in welcoming tones: 'Ah, our English *Zuster*! We are all glad that you are here, and we wish you a happy stay. Come, we will have coffee and then I will show you round. Doctor van Someren tells me that you are—are *bijdehand*,' she tried again, '*handig*', and Phoebe said quickly, 'Oh, I think you must mean handy.'

Zuster Witsma smiled. She had a round, friendly face and Phoebe guessed her to be about her own age. 'That you can do all things,' she explained happily as she offered Phoebe a mug of coffee across her desk. 'Now I will tell you all—day duty first, and then night duty every

four weeks—one week. We work from seven in
the morning until three o'clock on one day and
on the other day from two o'clock until ten in
the evening. The night nurses do duty from nine
in the evening until half past seven in the morning. You find the hours strange, yes? But they
work very well, you will see,' she nodded her
head encouragingly. 'There is always much to
do for the children; they depend on us to keep
them happy too, and Doctor van Someren will
not have that they are treated as sick. Even when
they are very ill he does not like that they should
know, only then we put them into the last ward—
but never until there is nothing more to do, you
understand.' Her blue eyes surveyed Phoebe.
'You are very pretty.'

'Thank you,' Phoebe smiled at the other girl,
liking her, finding herself looking forward to the
weeks of work ahead. 'Where would you like
me to start?'

The rest of the morning passed on wings; at
midday she went down to the basement, through
a labyrinth of passages and odd stairs, with some
of the other nurses, and ate her dinner with them
in a long dark room with a row of small windows
at one end, and listened to the chatter going on
around her, wishing she could understand at least
some of it, although everyone was very kind.
Some of the nurses spoke good English, all had
a smattering, and they took care to include her
in their conversations when they could. She went
back to the ward presently, to do the medicine
round with Zuster Witsma and be shown the

mechanism of admitting a patient, which was exactly the same as in an English hospital, and then to be initiated into the mysteries of writing the report, finally to be told kindly that she might go off duty. 'There will be things you wish to do,' said Zuster Witsma in a friendly voice, 'and perhaps a little walk, no? Tomorrow at two o'clock you will come again.'

Phoebe went off duty, conscious of a keen disappointment because she had seen no sign of Doctor van Someren; there had been a young doctor, who, before doing his round, had been introduced as Doctor Pontier, the Registrar. There were two other house doctors, he told her gravely, whom she would meet in due course, and he and they would be glad to help her in any way they could. He had smiled at her, openly admiring of her good looks, and had said with a flattering eagerness that he hoped that he would see more of her soon. She dismissed him from her thoughts as soon as she reached her room; it was already past three o'clock; she had intended to write a letter home, now she had the far better idea of telephoning. She changed out of her uniform and hurried out of the hospital and was on the point of opening its front door when a pretty blonde girl, also on her way out, stopped. 'The English nurse?' she asked cheerfully. 'You would like that I go with you and show the way?'

Her name was Petra—Petra Smit. She was, she told Phoebe rapidly in fluent, ungrammatical English, a trained nurse working on the surgical ward. 'We all hear about you,' she informed

Phoebe gaily, 'we hope that you will like us.'

Phoebe assured her that she would and went on to explain that she wanted to telephone. Half way through her explanation she put her hand to her mouth. 'Money!' she exclaimed. 'What a twit I am—I haven't any Dutch money. I never thought to change it before I left and then I didn't think about it. . .'

'Easy,' said her companion. 'The banks are closed, you understand, but there is a shop— they will take your English money.'

Phoebe got her money, and armed with it and still in the faithful Petra's company, she went to the Post Office where her companion, with pressing business of her own, left her, giving her instructions as to how to get back to the hospital before she did so, instructions which Phoebe immediately forgot in the excitement of speaking to Aunt Martha. But it was a small town, she told herself unworriedly as she strolled along in the warm sunshine, and when she saw a tea-room on the corner of two narrow streets, she went in, took a table in one of its windows, watching the people and bicycles crossing and re-crossing the complexity of canals and bridges while she drank her tea and then applied herself to the street map Petra had thoughtfully bought for her. Refreshed, she set off on a voyage of discovery—the Prinsenhof, she soon discovered, was a useful centre from which to find her way. She had peered into no more than half the shops around it when the city clocks reminded her that it was five o'clock and supper at the hospital was only

an hour away. She loitered along, peering down
the narrow streets and along the canals, each
lined with houses, some built into the water
itself. They were narrow and old, their gabled
roofs rising sharply, each with its tiny window at
the very top—she longed to explore one of them.

She played tennis after supper. Somewhere at
the back of the hospital a hard court had been
made in the square of ground around which the
greater part of the building was built. Someone
lent her a racquet, the evening was bright and
still warm, and they were evenly matched. The
four of them stood, getting their breaths before
they played a final set, and Phoebe peered up
at the windows around them, wondering which
belonged to Zaal Drie. She had given up hope
of finding it when a movement at one of the
windows caught her eyes. Doctor van Someren
was standing there, watching them. She looked
away quickly and when they began the next set,
her play, to her vexation, was indifferent, but at
the end of the game, when she stole another look,
he had gone. It was no comfort to her that she
played quite brilliantly during the next game.

She admitted to disappointment when she
didn't see him during the following day either,
for he had done a round, Zuster Witsma told her,
that morning, and although the Registrar came
during the afternoon, bringing one of the
housemen with him, and both young gentlemen
made themselves very pleasant to her, she went
down to her supper quite put out. That this was
a foolish attitude on her part she was the first to

admit. There was no reason why the doctor should make a point of seeing her; she had come to learn his methods—just as easily learned from Zuster Witsma and the medical staff—and he was, moreover, an important man in his own world—he had, to coin a phrase, other fish to fry.

She went back after supper and set about settling the children for the night. They were tired now, but some of them, despite this, were determined to stay awake as long as possible and tired though they were, couldn't settle. She thumped up pillows, rearranged bedclothes, squeezed oranges and as a last resort with one small boy, Dirk, who had worked himself into quite a state, lifted him out of his bed and sat him on her knee, and because she could think of nothing else to do, began to talk to him in English. That he couldn't understand a word didn't seem to matter; her voice was soothing and gentle, presently he chuckled, tucked his lint-fair head into her shoulder, and forgetting to wail, stared up at her with huge blue eyes. She tucked him a little closer; he was one of the ones who wasn't going to get well, so the Registrar had told her; he had been in hospital for almost a year, on and off, and Doctor van Someren had done wonders but it was a losing battle, although, he had hastened to add, several of the children went home much improved. One day they would cure all the children, he had said determinedly, and Phoebe, recalling Doctor van Someren's absorbed face when he was on his ward round, found herself agreeing, for she imagined him to be a quietly persistent man who didn't take no for an answer.

She winked a gorgeous long-lashed eye at Dirk and looked up to see the man she was thinking about standing beside them. She hadn't heard him come into the ward, probably because she hadn't expected him. She was still deciding what to say when he said 'Hullo, Phoebe,' and added something in his own language, and when she asked in a whisper what it was he had said he shook his head and smiled. 'All alone?' he asked.

'Yes, but only for a short time—Zuster Witsma's gone to supper and the night staff will be here shortly.'

He sat down on the edge of Dirk's bed. 'You think you will like it here?'

She nodded. 'Yes, very much—I felt a bit lost yesterday and today. . .' There was faint reproach in her voice although she was unaware of it, but he must have heard it, for he said at once: 'I do a good deal of work at Leyden—the Medical School is there, as you know, but I contrive to come here at least once a day, twice if necessary—sometimes more often. I must confess I like working here, although a more out-of-date place would be hard to find.'

'But it's beautifully equipped.'

He nodded a little absently, staring ahead of him and frowning. Presently he asked: 'You're comfortable in the Nurses' Home? I'm afraid you can't qualify for the Sisters' quarters.'

She flushed. 'That's quite all right. I knew I'd be working as a staff nurse. I don't deserve it anyway. My room is very comfortable and everyone is kind to me.'

He got to his feet, took the sleepy Dirk from her and laid him in his bed. His good night was abrupt and she stared after his broad back in surprise, wondering if she had said something to annoy him.

She was on duty at seven o'clock the next morning, and when Zuster Witsma came on at eight, she did the medicine round with her again, studied a case history with an eye to Doctor van Someren's methods, and then listened to the Ward Sister's painstaking explanations of the smallest detail to do with running the ward before going down to the dining room for her coffee. She was half way through the ward door when Zuster Witsma called her back.

'A little talk about your journey home for your sister's wedding,' she said kindly. 'Doctor van Someren has asked me to arrange that you have a sufficiency of free days—for such an important family event it is necessary that you have the maximum.' She led the way into her office, waved Phoebe to a chair and sat down at her desk. 'It is easy,' she went on, refreshing her memory from the odds and ends of forms, notebooks and folders before her. 'You will do the night duty—seven nights, and then you will have five nights in which to make your trip.'

She beamed across at Phoebe and Phoebe beamed back because she had been worrying as to how she should ask for the time off. Apparently Doctor van Someren wasn't so forgetful after all! 'That will be lovely,' she agreed. 'It's in a few weeks' time. . .'

'Just right; by then you will know the ward routine and you will have learned a little of Dutch, yes?'

Phoebe echoed the yes and hoped she would. It sounded an awful language, but perhaps by then she would have picked up an odd word or two—surely if everyone around her could speak at least a little English, she could do the same with Dutch. She remembered the dictionary in her uniform pocket and promised herself a little steady work with it each day.

She went to coffee then, wondering why Doctor van Someren hadn't seen fit to tell her that she would be able to go home—perhaps he considered it hardly his business; she was not a very important cog in the wheel of his scheme, and there was no reason for him to put himself out.

She was free that afternoon, she went out into the early June sun, determined to see as much as possible. Her guide book told her to go to the Markt, with its fourteenth-century New Church and its Town Hall, but although she started off in that direction, she quickly became diverted by a great many other things equally interesting. Shops for a start, little streets with old crooked houses which looked half forgotten, canals lined with trees and behind them, gracious houses with narrow flat fronts and heaven knows what treasures behind their solid doors. She strolled along, looking almost fragile in her sugar pink cotton

dress, oblivious of the admiring glances cast at
her as she walked. She had stopped to listen to
a street organ when a bunch of small boys came
tearing along, on their way home from school,
she supposed, stepping prudently against the
wall to give them room on the narrow pavement.
But they stopped, pushing and shoving and
fighting as small boys will, hemming her in
entirely, so that she came in for more than her
share of kicks and blows. Phoebe tucked her
handbag under her arm for greater safety and,
conscious of sore shins and trodden-on feet, gave
vent to her feelings.

'Oh, move on, do!' she apostrophised them
loudly. 'Quarrelsome brats, why don't you kick
each other's shins instead of mine?'

Naturally no one took any notice, at least,
none of them except one small boy of about eight
who had just fetched her an unintentional blow
with his school satchel—its buckle had etched
a weal above her wrist. They stared at each other
for a long moment and she realised with a shock
that he had understood what she had said. He
put his tongue out at her, shouted something
at his companions, and they all made off
together—a good thing, she thought crossly, for
her own tongue had itched to retort in kind.

The weal was still very much in evidence
when she went on duty the following morning.
Zuster Witsma, clucking sympathetically,
cleaned it up, but nothing could disguise the
nasty bruise around it. She had told everyone
that she had bumped into something and left it

at that, and when Doctor van Someren, with his
registrar and a posse of students entered the
ward, she took care to keep her hands behind
her back, just in case he might, for no reason at
all, want to know how she had come by it, and
she had no intention of telling him—she might
never see the little boy again, but that was no
reason to tell on him.

It was unfortunate that during the round she
should be asked to get one of the children ready
for examination, for the bruise, although she did
her best to conceal it, was very much in evidence;
but it wasn't until the round was over, the students bunched at the ward doors, the Registrar
standing a little apart and Doctor van Someren
standing in the middle of the ward having a few
words with Sister, that Phoebe, hanging up charts
and tidying beds and buttoning pyjama jackets,
saw Zuster Witsma look across the ward in her
direction and then walk towards her. She was
smiling largely, as though she were the bearer
of splendid news. 'Doctor van Someren wishes
to speak to you—in the office. Go quickly, Nurse
Brook, he is not to be kept waiting.'

Phoebe saw no reason to go quickly; it
smacked of being back at school, summoned to
the Head because she had been naughty, and as
usual, caught at it. The thought put her in mind
of the little boy; for some reason his angry face
with its thatch of fair hair had stayed in her
memory. She pushed open the door, feeling
faintly angry herself.

Doctor van Someren was standing by the

narrow window, his hands in his pockets, his attention apparently taken by the blank brick wall which was all the view there was, but he turned round as she went in and said without preamble: 'Ah, yes—you have a bruise on your arm. Why?'

And there's a silly question, thought Phoebe pertly. 'Something hit it,' she told him, the pertness in her voice.

He glanced at his watch and frowned. 'Do not waste my time, I beg of you, Miss Phoebe Brook; I am responsible for your person while you are here. I wish to be certain that the—er—something was reasonably clean.' He raised his eyes to her face. 'I am indifferent as to its cause; I have no wish to pry. . .'

Phoebe could feel her annoyance melting away. She caught at the shreds of it and said a little tartly: 'I'm quite capable of looking after myself, and you have no reason to worry, it was only a school s—the buckle of a bag—someone quite accidentally swung it against my arm. It's as clean as a whistle.'

He was staring at her with a kind of alert thoughtfulness which she found strangely disconcerting; just as though he had remembered something and was putting two and two together.

'Yes? Very well—but please take care; you are not to be replaced.'

She inched to the door. Of course she could be replaced, she knew of half a dozen nurses of her acquaintance who would jump at the chance of her job. She opened her mouth to say something, she wasn't sure what, but it didn't matter because he spoke first.

'Tomorrow you have a day off. I think that you should see the hospital at Leyden—the research department where I do most of my work. I have arranged with Zuster Witsma to bring you there in the afternoon.' He looked suddenly vague. 'Thank you, Nurse.'

She got herself out of the room, hardly knowing whether to be annoyed or laugh. Here he was, arranging her day off for her without a by-your-leave. Presumably she was supposed to be so mad keen on her work that she would welcome its spilling over into her free time. Upon thinking about it she was quite glad to have her day arranged for her; she had hardly had the time to plan any expeditions herself, and to tell the truth she was diffident about going around on her own until she had found out about buses and trains and the easiest way to get about.

Later that day, when she was off duty, she found her way to the VVV, a kind of tourist information centre which supplied leaflets and maps in a great many languages. Here she collected as many as possible about Leyden and went to bed early to study them in peace and quiet, and in the morning, making a leisurely dressing gown breakfast while her uniformed companions gobbled and swallowed against time, she contrived to add to what she had learned by asking a few questions about the hospital at Leyden. She sauntered back upstairs, sorting the facts from some of the more frivolous answers she had been given—the Medical School sounded interesting. She began to look forward to her afternoon, but in the meantime the morning stretched before her in delightful idleness. She dressed and wandered out into the bright morning, intent on finding somewhere pleasant for coffee while she decided how to spend the time before midday dinner.

She went, finally, to Reyndorp's Prinsenhof, where the prices rather took her breath away although the surroundings were worth every penny, and then went to look at Tetar van Elven Museum and afterwards, by way of light relief, window-shopped, a delightful pastime which culminated in the buying of a French silk scarf which she didn't really need but which was just too lovely to pass by.

They were to leave for Leyden directly after lunch, so that Phoebe spent half an hour before then changing her dress and attending to her face and hair. She chose the sugar pink cotton again because it seemed rather an occasion and crowned her bright head with a natural straw hat with a small upturned brim, and got out her nicest sandals and handbag. She was glad that she had done this when she saw Zuster Witsma waiting for her in her Daf. She had dressed for the occasion too—in blue and white; they made rather a nice pair, Phoebe considered as she got in beside her. The drive to Leyden was a short one of only a few miles, but Mies Witsma was a shocking driver so that the distance seemed twice that length. Phoebe made conversation in a voice which only shook slightly when they missed a bus by a hairsbreadth and again when Mies, seeing a dog about to cross the road, shot across into the path of the oncoming cars, causing a good deal of horn-blowing and squeaking of brakes. It was a decided relief when they entered Leyden and slowed down, and when they entered the Rapenburg, its quiet waters reflecting the great buildings on either side of it, Phoebe forgot about her companion's erratic driving and looked about her, trying to identify them as Zuster Witsma pointed them out—something which did her driving no good at all.

They had gone through the gates of the Medical School and were about to enter its door when Phoebe said: 'You do look nice—I hope you don't mind me saying so. . .'

The girl beside her turned a beaming face tinged with shy embarrassment. 'You think? I wish to be chic today—I hope he will think as you do. . .'

Phoebe was conscious of a peculiar sensation of doubt deep inside her—who was this *he*? Surely not Doctor van Someren? At the idea the feeling, now tinged with a slight peevishness, became stronger. She longed to ask and would have done so, but they were in the entrance hall by now and a young man was bearing down upon them.

He shook hands with Zuster Witsma, uttered a few words, presumably of welcome, and then turned to Phoebe, shook her hand too and said: 'Van Loon,' and she, wishing to be civil, told him: 'I'm Phoebe Brook,' then remembered that she was Sybil, or didn't that matter any more?

They walked the length of the hall while the young man, in quite beautiful English, explained that he was one of Doctor van Someren's team and had been sent to meet them, and when they fetched up before a massive mahogany door he tapped importantly and threw it open.

Phoebe hadn't known what she expected to see, certainly not Doctor van Someren stretched out in a comfortable chair by one of the long windows, fast asleep. The young man, not in the least put out, stepped forward, tapped him briskly on the shoulder and murmured deferentially, whereupon he opened his eyes and got to his feet and advanced to greet them, his manner imperturbable. Mies Witsma shook hands first, talking animatedly and at some length, and Phoebe watched narrowly, deciding that the doctor was certainly not the *he* her companion had mentioned. This filled her with such pleasure that it showed on her face and her host remarked: 'You look as though you had just made a delightful discovery—nothing to do with me taking a nap, I hope?'

She laughed. 'No, of course not—it seems an awful shame to wake you up, though. I'm sorry.'

He shrugged his great shoulders. 'It is a pleasure to wake and find you—and Zuster Witsma—here.' He looked over his shoulder to where the young man was deep in conversation with her. 'Van Loon,' he said easily, 'be a good chap and let Doctor Lagemaat know that we are ready, will you? And I will see you tomorrow as usual.'

Van Loon said, 'Yes, sir,' and then, 'Good-day, ladies, it has been a pleasure,' and cast a lingering look at Phoebe as he hurried away, to be replaced in no time at all by a very tall, very thin man, soberly dressed in dark grey and a rather dreary tie, but his face was pleasant and good-looking too in a blunt-featured way, and Phoebe, watching with quickening interest, saw at once that this was the one who was to be dazzled by the blue and white outfit. Zuster Witsma went pink as he came in and greeted him with the extreme casualness of manner which, to Phoebe at least, was all the proof she needed. He had smiled nicely at her as he crossed the room; he smiled nicely at her too as Doctor van Someren introduced him, but he went back immediately to the Dutch girl.

'We will go,' said Doctor van Someren, break-ing into her speculations. 'Arie, you will accompany Mies, will you not? and I will go with Miss Brook so that she misses nothing of what is to be seen.'

There was a great deal to be seen, and all very interesting too. Phoebe had never been keen on research, but she had to admit that it was a fascin-ating subject. The path lab engaged her attention too; she spent some considerable time peering down a microscope while the doctor patiently explained what she was looking at. When she finally got to her feet there was no sign of the others—they were alone at one end of the vast place and there was no one within earshot.

'Oh, dear,' said Phoebe, 'I've held everything up, haven't I? I'm sorry—I've kept everyone waiting.'

The doctor's voice sounded amused. 'My dear good girl, do you really suppose the other two have any idea as to what we are doing, or where we are? I credited you with an eye sharp enough to see that.'

She smiled at him and a dimple showed itself briefly. 'Oh, yes, I did, but I thought perhaps it was just me. Isn't that nice? She's such a dear and he looks rather a sweetie, only I don't like his tie.'

He let out a great shout of laughter. 'Do your suitors stand or fall by virtue of the ties they choose?' he wanted to know.

'I haven't got any s...' She stopped, remembering Jack.

'What's his name?' enquired her companion with an intentness quite at variance with his usual placid manner, and she found herself answering obediently: 'Jack—only he's not my—my suitor, not really, just persistent.'

They walked out of the path lab and started down a long wide corridor.

'Will he be at the wedding?' her companion wanted to know, and his voice was very soft.

'No—yes, I don't know.' She gave him a bewildered look and encountered his eyes; the gleam in them left her even more bewildered and strangely excited. She turned her head away and said, a little breathless. 'Where are we going now?'

'The small museum attached to the school— some fascinating things there—and we have just time. . .'

Phoebe peeped at him. He resembled himself again, not the exciting man who had stared at her so strangely a moment ago. She said primly: 'I hope we haven't taken up too much of your time.'

He flung open a door and started down a steep flight of steps beside her. 'No.' He opened the door at the bottom and ushered her into the museum. Mies Witsma and his colleague Arie were there, staring at an old engraving of some medieval gentleman having his leg amputated and, from the look on his face, taking grave exception to it. Phoebe doubted if either of them saw that, though; they looked up with the slightly bewildered air of people who have been interrupted unnecessarily but are too polite to say so, and her companion must have seen that too, for he made no attempt to join them, merely saying: 'We'll see you both in five minutes in the front hall,' and led her away in the opposite direction.

'I can't possibly see all this in five minutes,' began Phoebe.

'No—but I want my tea. I'll show you the most important exhibits, you shall come again and see the rest.'

She was hurried from one case to the next and whisked through the door again with her impressions nicely muddled and feeling hurt because he seemed in such a hurry to finish their tour. There was a great deal she hadn't seen, she felt sure—what about the wards and theatres and. . .

'Tea!' boomed Doctor van Someren from somewhere above her, and hurried her along more passages until they emerged in the front hall once more. The other two were there already. 'Coming with us?' he asked them. 'Arie, you take the Daf, I'll take Phoebe with me.' He started down the steps, his hand firmly on her arm.

'I haven't said goodbye,' she protested.

'Quite useless,' he told her cheerfully, 'and unnecessary. You will see them very shortly. Come along.'

'Where to?'

He stopped short. 'Did I not invite you? No, I see that I didn't. You are all coming to tea at my house.'

'At your house?' She was aware that her conversation lacked sparkle, but he was going a little fast for her.

'Yes, of course—why not?'

He was crossing the courtyard to where the Jaguar waited sleekly, and she found herself forced to trot in order to keep up with him.

'I'm not sure that I should,' she essayed. 'It's such a great waste of your time, and whatever will your wife think if you bring hordes of people back for tea?'

'Not hordes,' he corrected her, 'three, and I have no wife.'

She got into the car because he had opened its door and obviously expected her to, pity and sympathy swelling inside her—poor man, so he was a widower, or divorced—although she couldn't think how any woman in her right senses would want to let a man like him go once she had him. . . What a life it must be for him, bringing up a small boy. Someone had told her that children didn't go to boarding school in Holland—perhaps there was a governess. She stifled a pang of disquiet at the thought; someone young and pretty, who might catch her companion unawares and marry him. Her reflections were interrupted by his quiet voice: 'Who told you that I was married?'

'Someone in England—at least, they didn't say that you were married, but that you had a son.' She turned to smile at him and encountered a faintly mocking smile.

'Hardly the same thing,' he murmured, and before she could recover: 'Did you enjoy this afternoon?'

She flushed, sensing his gentle snub. 'Very much,' she told him politely, and went on to enlarge upon the things she had seen until they were back in Delft where Doctor van Someren stopped the car in one of the narrow streets bordering a tree-lined canal, sending her heart into her mouth as they came to a halt, the car's elegant nose poised over the dark water.

'How often do cars get driven into the canals?' Her voice was tart to cover her fright.

He shrugged. 'Daily—we have an excellent rescue service, though.'

Which made her laugh as she got out to inspect the houses crowding on either side of the canal. She had wandered down that very street only that morning; it pleased her mightily that he was leading the way to one of them—a narrow house, five stories high, with a semi-basement and a double step leading to its front door. Inside the hall was cool and quiet and dim but not gloomy, for above their heads she could see a circular window set in the roof, towards which the narrow staircase wound, its carved balustrade forming a narrow spiral at each ascending gallery. The room they entered was cool too, the furniture old and simple and very beautiful, highlighted by the silver in a display cabinet against one wall and the paintings on its white walls. Phoebe halted in the middle of the room and said in a pleased voice:

'That's a Quaker chest, isn't it?' and then bit her lip because she had sounded rude, but her companion looked pleased.

'Yes—isn't it delightful? And how nice that you know it for what it is. You like old things?'

'Very much. I came past these houses this morning and longed to see inside them, and now I am—I can't believe my good luck.' She smiled, her sapphire eyes sparkling, and he said quickly: 'In that case. . .'

He got no further, for the door opened and Zuster Witsma and Doctor Lagemaat came in, followed almost immediately by a pleasant-faced woman whom Phoebe took to be the housekeeper, bearing a tray of tea things. She had hardly closed the door behind her when it was opened again and a small boy came in—the boy who had put his tongue out at her. He shot her a look of horrified surprise and ran across the room to Doctor van Someren, who had apparently not seen the look and said easily in English: 'Hullo, Paul—you must speak English for a little while, for we have a guest for tea—from England. Come and be introduced.'

Phoebe offered a hand and smiled. Little boys were, after all, little boys and what was a rude gesture between friends, but although he shook her hand and said how do you do with perfect good manners, the look he shot at her for the second time was far from friendly, rather was it suspicious and wary. She made a few random remarks to cover what she felt to be an awkward pause and was thankful when Paul went to talk to Mies Witsma and Doctor Lagemaat, with whom, she noted, he appeared to be on the best of terms. They had tea then, and everyone talked a great deal save for her host, who spoke so little she wondered if he were in danger of falling asleep again; apparently not, for the moment the meal was finished he sent Paul away to get on with his homework and offered to show her the house.

The next hour was a delight, for her host's idea of showing her round was to let her roam at will, merely opening and shutting doors as required, supplying the history of anything she enquired about, and putting into her hands some of his more delicate treasures for her to admire more closely. The size of the house surprised her, for it had great depth, with three rooms, one behind the other on the ground floor and some enchanting passages running haphazardly from the galleries above. There was a walled garden too, sloping down to another, smaller canal at the back of the house; it had a small jetty and a rowing boat, and at Phoebe's questioning look, the doctor said: 'Paul's—it's a safer way of getting around than the streets.'

She nodded, wondering about him and Paul. The boy was devoted to him, she had seen that at once, and the doctor seemed equally fond of Paul, but surely they didn't see much of each other? The doctor was engrossed in his work—ward rounds, teaching rounds, lectures, research work—there was no end to it; there couldn't be much time in which to be with the boy. 'He must have a lot of friends,' she ventured.

They were standing side by side, looking down into the dark water, highlighted here and there by the late afternoon sun. Her companion didn't answer this remark, instead he flung an arm around her shoulders. 'I hope you will be happy here,' he observed thoughtfully, and then to shock her into a gasp: 'You had met before, I gather.'

'Who?'

'Don't prevaricate, you're too sensible for that. You and Paul.' And when she didn't reply: 'Of course, this. . .' He took his arm away and lifted her hand to look at the still colourful bruise.

'A school satchel—that was what you intended to say, was it not? Very nice of you not to—how do you say—split? Although of course you had no idea who he was.'

'None,' she said faintly.

'But you could have said something just now.'

Phoebe snatched her hand away. 'Who do you take me for?' she asked crossly. 'I'm not in the habit of telling tales, you can't have a very good opinion of me.'

'As to that, it is a subject which, for the moment, I am not prepared to discuss.'

She looked at him then. 'What do you mean? Is it because I pretended to be Sybil?'

He looked amused. 'What an enquiring mind you have! I hope you are satisfied with the arrangements made for your visit to your home?'

A snub which she ignored because she was suddenly stricken. 'Oh, I forgot to thank you— I'm so grateful, it's exactly right, and Zuster Witsma says it won't upset anything at all.' She added a little shyly: 'You must find it very silly of me to wish to go home so soon after I've arrived here, but they wanted to get married before Nick took up this new job. . .'

'Naturally,' he agreed lazily, 'I think. . .'

She wasn't to know what he thought; the housekeeper came down the garden and began to speak to him in an urgent voice. He listened without speaking, nodded, said to Phoebe: 'I'm sorry, I have to return to the hospital immediately,' and started to walk back to the house.

'One of ours?' hazarded Phoebe, trying to keep up.

He didn't slacken his pace. 'One of ours, dear girl. You will forgive me?'

She nodded and stopped trying to keep pace with him. 'Thank you for a pleasant afternoon,' she said swiftly, and he turned to smile at her as he went.

Indoors she found the other two sitting close together in the small sitting room which opened into the garden. They had obviously been undisturbed for some time, and when she told them that the doctor had been called away and she would wait in the garden until they were ready to leave, they agreed with such an unflattering readiness that she made haste to go back to the garden. There was someone else there now—Paul, sitting in his boat, doing something or other to one of the oars.

She went and stood close by him and ignoring the scowl on his little face, said coaxingly: 'You understand English very well, don't you, Paul, well enough for you to understand me when I say that I should like to be friends? I don't care a row of buttons about the other afternoon, you know—indeed, I'd forgotten about it. Couldn't we be friends?'

He didn't smile, but at least he seemed interested. He was on the point of speaking when his eyes slid past hers, watching someone coming down the garden. Phoebe turned to see who it was—a girl, tall and dark and magnificently eye-catching. She wasn't hurrying; by the time she reached them Phoebe had the unpleasant feeling that she had been studied from head to toes, assessed, and instantly disliked. Nonetheless, the girl's manners were charming. 'You don't know who I am, so I'll introduce myself—I should have been home for tea, but I was held up by the traffic. I'm Maureen Felman, Paul's governess. You're the English nurse, aren't you? Lucius told me about you.'

'Lucius?' Phoebe forced her voice to friendliness. 'Do you mean Doctor van Someren?'

The girl laughed. 'I forgot—I've been here so long, we've been Lucius and Maureen for years.'

Phoebe let that pass. 'My name's Phoebe Brook. Your English is so good you must be. . .'

'My mother. I speak both languages fluently.' And Phoebe, already disliking her, disliked her still more for the smugness of her voice. 'Paul and I speak English when we're together— Lucius wants that.'

'Paul's English is very good,' observed Phoebe politely. 'Do you live here?'

'Not yet.' Maureen smiled as she spoke; the smile was smug too and Phoebe's dislike turned to instant hate. 'Lucius is a stickler for the conventions—I live here during the day, though, and while Paul's at school I act as secretary to Lucius and drive him around when he doesn't want to drive himself.'

Phoebe murmured a casual something; it would never do to let this girl think that she was even faintly interested in the doctor. All the same, she found it strange that he liked to be driven. He had struck her as a man who did his own driving, and what secretarial work was there for her to do? There was a secretary at the hospital, who did the ward rounds with him, she had seen that with her own eyes—was this girl hinting that she was something more to him than a secretary-cum-governess? She glanced at Paul and saw that he was watching her in a speculative way which caused her to say airily: 'It sounds a nice job. I hope we meet again before I go back to England.'

'Probably—Delft is small. You must come round one day and Paul shall practise his English on you.' She gave the little boy a malicious glance as she spoke and Phoebe had the uncomfortable feeling that she didn't like him—and she must be on very close terms with the doctor if she could invite people to his house... She said sweetly: 'How nice. I shall look forward to that, and now I must go and find Zuster Witsma.'

That young lady was, in fact, advancing down the garden at that very moment. She spoke coolly to Maureen, with warmth to Paul and swept Phoebe away. 'Doctor Lagemaat has to be back—we'll drop you off at St Jacobius as we go,' she explained.

They paused for a moment before they entered the house and looked back. Paul and his governess were standing watching them, and Maureen was laughing, they could hear the light mocking sound quite clearly.

In the car Mies turned in her seat to say: 'Not nice, that girl, but clever. Doctor van Someren thinks that she is a splendid governess and of such great help to him.' She snorted: 'He is so wrapped up in his work he can see nothing!'

Outside the hospital, when Doctor Lagemaat stopped the car, he turned to say to her: 'We must not bother you with our small differences of opinion, but we are old friends of Doctor van Someren, and I agree with Mies.' He smiled nicely at her. 'May I not call you Phoebe?'

'Oh, please,' said Phoebe instantly, and Mies chimed in: 'And you shall call me Mies—not in the hospital, of course, and him,' she nodded at Doctor Lagemaat, 'you shall call Arie. Thus we shall be friends!'

Phoebe, standing on the pavement, watching them drive away, felt a pleasant warmth. It was nice to make friends; it was nice, too, to know that Lucius van Someren had good friends too. She had a sudden urge to find out as much as possible about him.

# CHAPTER FOUR

SHE had her opportunity the very next day, for in the morning, when Doctor van Someren had finished his teaching round, he clove his way through the circle of students to where she was standing behind Mies, and said: 'I have a few hours to spare this afternoon—you will be free, I take it? I should like you to visit the Hortus Botanicus behind the university, and should there be time to spare, another visit to the museum might not come amiss.'

Phoebe thanked him quietly, conscious of a pleasurable glow beneath her starched apron, and when he went on: 'At the entrance, then, at half past three,' she had a job not to smile widely with the pleasure she felt; instead she said soberly enough: 'Very well, sir,' and received a little grunt in reply as he wandered away. She watched him go down the ward; at the door he stopped to write in his notebook and she wondered what it could be—a reminder perhaps, about the afternoon's outing.

She was a little late, for it hadn't been possible to get off duty punctually and she had had to change much too quickly, so that she was totally dissatisfied with her appearance as she hurried to the hospital entrance. Nonetheless, she looked cool and fresh in her blue and white striped dress, and because it was unusually hot for the time of year, she had dispensed with stockings and put on a pair of blue sandals which exactly matched her shoulder bag. But if she had hoped for a word of appreciation from her companion she was to be disappointed; he gave her the briefest of greetings and hardly looked at her. They were free of Delft and well on the way to Leyden when he said: 'I'm sorry I had to leave you yesterday afternoon.'

'It didn't matter at all,' she assured him, 'especially as Wil is so much better today—it was for her you went, wasn't it?'

He nodded and she went on, choosing her words: 'I went back to the garden after you left, just for a little while—Paul was there, and then his governess came.'

'Maureen? Ah, yes, she mentioned that she had met you. She organises us—a most efficient girl.'

'And a very striking one,' remarked Phoebe, hoping he would go on talking about the wretched creature if she gave him a little encouragement. But she was frustrated by his: 'You can afford to be generous, Phoebe,' a remark which pinkened her cheeks with annoyance, because what might have been meant as a compliment had been uttered in a tone of voice which verged on mockery. The vague half thoughts she had had of putting a spoke in Maureen's wheel withered away under the sudden sideways glance he directed at her—not in the least absent-minded but very intent, as though he knew what was in her mind. The pink deepened and she looked out of the window and made an observation, stiffly, about the weather. She was sorry she had come, she told herself savagely, and how stupid of her to allow her interest to settle upon a man she was unlikely to see again once she had gone back to England and who was already quite satisfied with his life, and anyway, a small stern voice reminded her, was it quite sporting to try and attract his attention away from the glamorous Maureen? She had no opportunity of solving this interesting problem, because they had arrived at the Medical School once more and her companion was suggesting, in the mildest of voices, that she should get out of the car.

The next hour was a delight to her. They wandered round slowly, and Phoebe, naming each plant as they inspected it, was quite taken aback when Doctor van Someren exclaimed: 'Good heavens, girl, your Latin is excellent—are you a botanist as well as a nurse?'

She denied it, suddenly shy. 'Why, no—my father was, at least it was his hobby. We used to go for walks and he taught me a great deal.'

'Latin or botany?' he asked idly.

'Both, I suppose.'

'What profession had your father?'

She bent to examine a fine specimen of basil. 'He was a scientist.'

They had reached a fine old mulberry tree with a bench built around it. 'Let us sit,' suggested the doctor. 'The museum can wait until another day—you shall tell me about your father and something of yourself too, and I shall discover even more facets to your character.'

She was taken aback. 'Facets? Whatever for—I didn't know I had any.'

They were sitting side by side and the sunlight dribbled through the leaves on to her bright hair. He answered her quietly: 'Oh, you have a great many—you are intelligent for a start, you have a quick brain, you are kind, impulsive—you like your own way.' He went on, ignoring her gasp: 'I think you may have a nasty temper when you are roused. You are intensely curious. . .,

'What about?' she demanded.

'Me,' he answered simply.

'I'm not,' she began, and he said sharply, 'and do I have to add another facet—a slight twisting of the truth?'

'Well, what if I am?' she snapped crossly. 'It's natural, and at least I haven't turned you into facets like a specimen under your microscope, sir.'

'Ah, yes—something I had forgotten to mention. Would you refrain from addressing me as sir? My name is Lucius; I do not propose that you should address me so in hospital, but surely when we are away from our work we might assume that we are friends. I am not so very much older than you, Phoebe.' And at her look of surprise: 'Thirty-four, and you are twenty-seven.'

'How you do harp on my age,' she protested. 'It's not nice to remind a woman how old she is '

He lifted colourless eyebrows 'Indeed? Have

I offended you? I'm sorry.' He didn't look in the least sorry; he was laughing at her. After a moment she smiled reluctantly and he said instantly: 'That's better—don't you want to ask me any questions?'

She said without hesitation: 'Yes, of course I do, but it wouldn't be polite.'

His blue eyes twinkled. 'Try me, or shall I answer the first one for you? You wonder about Paul, do you not? He calls me Papa and you have been told that I have a son, and where, you ask yourself, is his wife—dead, divorced, run away with some other man who has no work to fill his days and more money than he knows what to do with?' He paused. 'Yes?'

'Yes,' said Phoebe, thinking how very good-looking he was.

'I have no wife—Paul is my adopted son. His parents—my friends—died in that Italian plane crash four or five years ago—perhaps you remember it? I am his godfather, he has no grandparents; it was right and natural that he should make his home with me.'

The flood of relief she felt quite shocked her. Not stopping to think, she said: 'Oh, I thought— that is, I. . .'

'I have no doubt you did,' he agreed suavely. 'I should have mentioned it to you before, but it slipped my memory.'

She disagreed quite fiercely. 'Oh, no, why should you? It's none of my business,' and felt irrationally disappointed at the casual shrug he gave in answer. They sat in silence then, the breeze stirring the tree above them, the air full of the varied hum of insects.

'All the live murmur of a summer's day,' uttered the doctor suddenly.

'Matthew Arnold,' Phoebe gave the information automatically and then laughed when he said: 'You are a difficult girl to impress—your knowledge of botany is more than satisfactory, so is your Latin, and now, when I quote an apt phrase, you cap it with its author.'

'Oh, I'm sorry—I didn't mean to—I wasn't trying to impress you or anything.' She added earnestly: 'As a matter of fact, I hardly know any.'

'No? I shall have to try and catch you out.' He gave her a long considering look which so disconcerted her that she suggested that they should finish their tour of the garden.

'You'll come back with me to tea?' he asked her as they got into the car later.

She hadn't expected that and it flustered her. 'Me? Well—I came yesterday.'

He shot the car with heart-stopping precision between a slow-moving lorry and a stationary baker's cart. 'I hadn't forgotten,' he told her mildly. 'I thought it would be pleasant for you to further your acquaintance with Maureen, and it's good for Paul to speak English as much as possible.'

'Why?'

'He wants to go to Oxford. His father and I were there, you see.'

Paul and Maureen were in the garden, sitting

on the grass and although the boy ran to greet the doctor and give a hand to Phoebe, his governess made no effort to rise. Only when they had reached her she lifted her head and smiled at them with a casual hello and an offer to fetch the tea into the garden. 'It's so warm,' she explained. 'When Paul came out of school we decided that the garden was the only place to be. I hope you agree, Lucius?' She looked at the doctor, who said vaguely: 'Oh, yes—do whatever is fun for Paul,' and then to the small boy hanging on his arm: 'The rowlock is loose in the boat. Have you seen it? We'll fix it now.'

So Phoebe was left alone to sit on the grass and admire the view and the flowers and watch the two of them absorbed in their work, their lint-fair heads close together. But not for long, for the doctor looked up, said something to Paul and got out of the boat to cast himself down beside her.

'Forgive me, I thought Maureen was here.'

'If you remember she went into the house to fetch the tea tray.'

He looked surprised. 'Did she? Well, why not—it's just the day to have tea out here.'

Phoebe suppressed a smile. 'Don't let me hinder you from mending whatever it is,' she reminded him.

'Paul can manage on his own now, I showed him what to do.' He rolled over to look at her. 'What do you intend to do with your evening?'

She was aware of intense pleasure, although she kept her voice carefully casual. 'Why. . .' she began, but was interrupted by Maureen, calling gaily for the doctor to go and carry the tray. He got to his feet with no sign of disappointment at not having had an answer, and by the time he had returned and they had settled to their tea, she could see that he had forgotten all about it.

Getting ready for bed that night, she decided that, from her point of view, the tea party had been a failure. Maureen had been charming, she had also been possessive towards the doctor— no, bossy, Phoebe corrected herself as she brushed her hair with unnecessary vigour. She had also managed, with diabolical sweetness, to put Phoebe in the wrong on several minor points during their conversation, and worse, made her out to be a little stupid as well. 'I hate her!' declared Phoebe a trifle wildly, and flung the brush across the room, which did it no good at all, but certainly relieved her pent-up feelings. And Paul had enjoyed her discomfiture too, staring at her with his sharp dark eyes. Only the doctor had been unaware, sitting there, making gentle talk and seeing to their wants. He was an exasperating man!

She went to the mirror and peered at her face without conceit; she was a very pretty girl, accustomed to being looked at at least twice, her voice was quiet and low, she neither giggled or laughed brassily. If she was a little shy, she took care to conceal it. There was nothing, she told her reflection, to which Doctor van Someren could take exception, if indeed he had ever taken the trouble to really look at her.

She got into bed. 'It's a pity nothing ever happens to me,' she told the ceiling, then closed her eyes and went to sleep, and Fate, who had overheard the remark, grinned impishly and went off to make her own arrangements.

It was a glorious morning and Phoebe was free until two o'clock. There was a great deal of the small city she hadn't seen and she took herself off to the Convent of St Agatha, where William the Silent had met his death, and this expedition over, and with time to spare, she decided to wander round one or two of the narrow streets leading away from the prescribed route to the hospital. The houses here were small, their walls uneven with age, their windows small too and filled with flowerpots so that Phoebe was unable to catch a glimpse of their interiors. They were neatly kept, with fresh paint and sparkling windows and here and there a canary bird singing in its cage hung outside an upstairs window. She wandered on, knowing herself to be lost but not worried, because Delft wasn't large enough for her to remain so; she would soon find her way again. She was on the point of doing this when her eye was caught by a cul-de-sac, lined with very small houses indeed, its cobbled centre ornamented by a plane tree. It was very quiet there and although the houses looked well tended, she had the strong impression that the place was empty. She had walked down one side of it and was about to cross over to the other when the door of a house she was passing opened, revealing a very old lady.

Phoebe paused in her walk, smiled, essayed the *'Dag, mevrouw'*, she had learned to say and prepared to move on, but a timid hand was laid on her arm and the old lady started to unburden herself at such length and with so much agitation that there was no use in Phoebe trying to stop her. When she at last came to an end they stood looking at each other in a puzzled way, Phoebe because she had no idea what the old lady wanted, the old lady because she was getting no response.

At length Phoebe said regretfully with a strong English accent: *'Niet verstaan,'* and then with a flash of inspiration asked: 'Help?'

The old lady nodded, muttered, *'Ja, ja, hulp!'*, and drew Phoebe inside. In the small overfurnished, spotlessly clean front room was another old lady, lying on the floor, her eyes closed. Phoebe lost no time in taking her pulse, which was far too weak for her peace of mind, just as the pale old face was far too white, and her breathing was so shallow that there was almost no movement of the old-fashioned black bodice. She was unconscious, but Phoebe was sure it wasn't a coronary, not even a black-out, but the old lady was ill, without a doubt. She selected a beautifully embroidered satin cushion from an assortment on the stiff settee and placed it beneath the old lady's head, then mimed the need for a blanket, reflecting that ignorance of the Dutch language was putting her at a most appalling disadvantage. The blanket was fetched, she tucked her patient up carefully, took her pulse again, peered under the closed eyelids and then once more played her desperate charade to convince her companion that she would have to go for help. This, naturally enough, took time, but once she had made herself understood, Phoebe wasted no time. She shot through the front door and began to run in the general direction of the St Bonifacius hospital. Lucius van Someren would be doing his round, she was quite certain of that, for whatever else he forgot, he didn't forget his patients. She could explain to him quickly, far more quickly than trying to find a policeman, or for that matter, any passer-by—and there were none at that moment—and wasting time making herself understood.

She got there quicker than she had hoped, because she chanced her luck, taking what looked like a short cut down a narrow alley and arriving almost in the hospital yard. She didn't stop to wonder what everyone would think as she belted up the stairs and into the ward. She hardly noticed the surprised faces or the children's quickened interest, only Lucius' calm face and his quiet: 'You want me, Phoebe?'

She nodded, out of breath. 'There's an old lady,' she began, and prayed that he wouldn't waste time asking questions, 'in a little house in the Breegsteeg,' she knew her pronunciation was awful, but she was past caring. 'She's ill— unconscious. I don't think it's a coronary—there wasn't anyone, only another old lady, and I didn't know where to get help, so I came to you.'

She looked at his grave, kind face and if she hadn't been so taken up with her errand, might have noticed the expression which passed over it. 'I'm sorry to interrupt the round.'

He asked no questions at all, but said something to Doctor Lagemaat who was with him and then: 'We'd better go and have a look, hadn't we?' and was off down the stairs, with Phoebe, still blown, trying to keep up with him.

In the car she repeated her apology, because to drag a consultant from his ward round—and now she came to think about it, there had been a crowd of students there, so it had been a teaching round—was hardly the thing. She added matter-of-factly: 'I'm sorry if you're annoyed. . .it's not knowing the language.'

He made a sound which could have been a laugh as he inched the Jaguar through the busy streets with no sign of impatience while she, with something of an effort, held her hands quiet in her lap, thanking heaven that the journey was so short.

The old lady was at the door, looking more bewildered than ever; Doctor van Someren paused briefly to speak to her and went inside, Phoebe close behind him, crowding into the small room. Presently, when he had made his examination, he said: 'You were right, it isn't a coronary—her skin's dry, she's very pale, not grey, just pale, and look at this.' He nodded at the bony arm he was holding. 'Malnutrition, general debility and anaemia, I should suppose,

but I'll leave that for the medical side to confirm.
Let's get her to hospital.'

Phoebe's lovely eyes asked a silent question.

'Yes, she'll get better—good food, rest, ferri.
sulph. . .'

'And the other lady, what's to happen to her?'

He smiled fleetingly. 'Her younger sister, a
mere eighty-two. We'll take her along with us
and get the social workers busy.'

'Why are they alone? Where's everyone?
Why haven't they enough money to. . .'

His smile widened. He said patiently: 'Not so
fast! They're alone because everyone living in
the *steeg* has gone on an outing, but our patient
didn't feel up to it, so they stayed behind—presumably she collapsed.' He got to his feet. 'Now,
let's get them to St Jacobus.'

They went in the car, Phoebe supporting the
unconscious patient on the back seat, her sister,
in her respectable, old-fashioned black coat and
hat, sitting in front. Phoebe listened to her dry
old voice, talking continuously now that relief
had loosened her tongue and the doctor's calm
tones had quietened her fright. She couldn't
understand a word of what was being said, but
she was quite confident that he would arrange
everything to everyone's satisfaction. He certainly had instant attention at the hospital; with a
brief direction that she was to stay in the waiting
room with the old lady, he disappeared with the
stretcher, a houseman, a couple of porters and a
rather fierce-looking Sister. He didn't come back
for twenty minutes, and Phoebe, looking up from

her efforts to comfort her weeping companion, said, faintly accusing: 'She needs a nice cup of tea. . .'

'Coffee,' he corrected her. 'We'll all have some, but first I must explain everything to her.' He took a chair and sat down by the old lady and began to talk to her. He sounded reassuring, and presently the old lady wiped her eyes, smiled a little and allowed him to help her to her feet. 'Now we'll go home,' he told Phoebe, 'and have that coffee and then take her back. She's to come and see her sister this afternoon—I've got someone to fetch her and take her back.' He paused. 'I suppose you're dying of curiosity—I'll explain it all to you later.'

She bristled. 'There's no need to put yourself out,' she said haughtily. Really, he was a most irritating man! Why had she ever rushed to him for help and dragged him away from his round and been so sure that he wouldn't be annoyed at the interruption? Vague notions about this floated at the back of her mind, but it was hardly the time to indulge in introspective thoughts. She got into the car with the old lady beside her, and was driven to the doctor's house.

It wasn't yet twelve o'clock. The hateful Maureen had told her that she spent her mornings in typing letters for the doctor, making appointments, filing correspondence and other secretarial duties. She had made it sound very important and Phoebe, despite herself, had been impressed, so that when the doctor opened the door and ushered them inside, she expected to hear the steady tap-tap of a typewriter, or failing that, the utter hush surrounding someone concentrating upon desk work. She heard neither—gales of laughter, the discordant thunder of a lesser-known pop group belting out a number on a record player, and the unmistakable clink of glasses were the sounds which assailed her astonished ears. But if she was astonished, her host was thunderstruck. His mouth thinned ominously, and it struck her suddenly that probably he had a shocking temper which he seldom allowed anyone to see. They weren't to see it now; after the barest pause, he led them to the sitting room, begged them to make themselves comfortable, pulled the bell rope with restrained violence and walked to the window to stare out into the street.

It was the housekeeper who answered it and Phoebe, who rather liked her, felt sorry for the surprise and discomfiture she was obviously experiencing. But her master ignored this, merely asking her to bring coffee, adding something else which Phoebe couldn't understand. Then he went and sat by the old lady and made gentle conversation.

But not for long, the door was opened presently and Maureen, rather pale, stood in the doorway, whereupon he got to his feet, saying in English: 'Ah, yes, Maureen—an explanation is due to me, I fancy—perhaps you will give it to me now.' He looked briefly at Phoebe. 'You will excuse me? And be good enough to pour the coffee when it comes.'

His voice, which he had neither raised nor quickened, was steely. Phoebe, feeling meanly delighted at Maureen's discomfiture, murmured suitably as she watched them leave the room together, then turned her attention to the old lady, who, unaware of any undercurrents, was smiling quite happily and, Phoebe very much feared, was about to embark upon an unintelligible conversation with her.

The coffee came. She attended to her companion's wants, poured herself a cup and listened to the sounds on the other side of the door—subdued voices, feet, a giggle quickly suppressed, and then utter silence. The visitors had gone. Somewhere in the house, behind one of the handsome doors, Doctor van Someren was with Maureen. Phoebe would dearly have loved to have been in a position to peer through the keyhole, or even eavesdrop. . . She gathered her straying thoughts together, appalled at the depths to which she had sunk. She had been well brought up; such actions were despicable, she reminded herself, and applied herself to the pouring of second cups, then as the doctor came into the room, filled a cup for him too, and because his mouth was set so very grimly and no one spoke, she began a one-sided conversation to which neither of her companions replied. She was aware that she sounded chatty, but they couldn't sit there for ever, saying nothing.

'A lovely day,' she ventured, having exhausted the excellence of the coffee. 'How early summer is this year,' and then losing patience, she snapped: 'It's a pity I can't speak Dutch, for then at least this lady here would understand me and make some sort of a civil answer.'

The doctor smiled then. 'Poor Phoebe! You have my deepest admiration. Here you are, longing, no doubt, to indulge your curiosity and forcing yourself to discuss the weather. It must be agony for you.' His blue eyes studied her reflectively. 'We're going to take Juffrouw Leen here home.'

Having said which he addressed himself to his other guest, who got to her feet, looking quite cheerful, and accompanied him to the door.

Outside Phoebe said stiffly: 'Well, I'll be getting along—thanks for the coffee.'

'You will come with us Phoebe—please.'

She got into the car again, telling herself that she was weak to do so, and when they arrived at the old lady's house, went inside, helped her off with her hat and coat and then waited patiently while Juffrouw Leen, possessing herself of the doctor's hand, began a long and voluble speech—thanking him, she supposed. Presently it was her own turn, but unlike the doctor, who had doubtless said something graceful, she was unable to do anything but smile. But Juffrouw Leen didn't seem to mind. She saw them off at the door, smiling and waving and quite happy again. Phoebe turned in her seat for a final farewell as they turned the corner of the *steeg* and Doctor van Someren said: 'The round will be finished. You're in time for your midday meal before you go on duty?'

'Yes, thank you. If you like to drop me off. . .'

He took no notice. Perhaps he hadn't heard, for he went on: 'Juffrouw Leen will be all right—a social worker will call each day to make sure she can manage and someone is lined up to take her to and from the hospital.'

'Her sister—will she do?'

'I think so—the right diet, rest, care, and someone to keep an eye on them when she's back home.' He glanced at her and smiled. 'I'm afraid your off duty has been sadly curtailed.'

'It didn't matter—I was only pottering.'

He drew up before St Bonifacius. 'You enjoy that?'

She nodded. 'Very much—in a few days I shall go further afield. I want to see all I can.'

He didn't answer but got out and opened the car door and went inside with her, bade her a brief goodbye and went up the stairs to the ward, and Phoebe, because there was nothing better to do, went down to the dining room and ate her dinner.

She was off duty again the next morning and she went along to see the old lady. There was someone with her—the district nurse, who had a smattering of English so that Phoebe was able to discover that the patient was doing quite well and that Juffrouw Leen was in good hands while her sister was in hospital. She stayed a while and had a cup of coffee with them, bade them a cheerful goodbye and made her way to the shops. She was coming out of Reynders, a piece of genuine blue Delftware tucked under her arm, when she came face to face with Maureen Felman, and before she could make up her mind whether to say a casual hallo and walk on, or stop and say a few polite words, Maureen had stopped, obviously intent on passing the time of day.

'Hullo,' she said coolly. 'I've been hearing all about you and your Nightingale act—I must say you don't look much like a do-gooder. Didn't you find it all a dead bore? Not that you'd be likely to say so.'

Phoebe eyed her thoughtfully. Here, she thought, was the enemy, although she wasn't quite sure why—and declaring war too.

'If I found it a dead bore,' she replied gently, 'I certainly wouldn't say so, but I didn't—I'm sure you would have done the same.'

Maureen smiled brilliantly. 'Not me—there are far too many old souls around as it is. I like life to be gay.' She stared at Phoebe and Phoebe looked back limpidly. 'You guessed that yesterday, I suppose.' Her eyes narrowed. 'Lucius never comes home before twelve o'clock—never—and yesterday, of all days...and you with him, all prunes and prisms! I could have managed him beautifully if you hadn't been there, looking as though butter wouldn't melt in your mouth. I was only having a few friends in for a drink—God knows life's dreary enough in that house.'

'You're rather rude,' Phoebe's voice had a decided edge to it, 'and I hardly know why, and what you choose to do while the doctor's away from home is really no concern of mine.' She smiled with charm. 'I dare say you're still feeling a bit scared—it must have been a nasty shock for you.' She allowed the smile to linger and watched Maureen's face tighten with ill temper. 'I must be going—it was interesting meeting you.'

She nodded and walked away briskly, thinking what a ghastly creature Maureen was and why, on the face of things, did the doctor put up with her. The thought that he might possibly be in love with her crossed her mind as it had done several times already, only now it refused to be dismissed. It remained, well damped down, for the rest of the day, affording her a good deal of disquiet.

It faded a little under the pressure of work during the next few days and even when she saw Doctor van Someren, it was always in the company of Mies Witsma or the other nurses, and their talk was entirely of the patients. It was the evening before her day off before she found herself alone with him; Zuster Witsma had gone to her supper, the ward was in the chaotic state which preceded the children's bedtime. Phoebe, with another nurse, was urging the more active and reluctant of her small patients to start undressing, supervising the washing of faces, the tidying of beds, the comforting of those who were feeling sorry for themselves and engaging, in her own peculiar, sparse Dutch, those who wished to talk in idle conversation. She had, naturally enough, become a little untidy during the carrying out of these tasks—her lovely hair was coming down, her nose shone, her apron was soaked with most of a glass of lemonade which a recalcitrant small boy had flung at her. Her pleasure at seeing him, therefore, was tinged with fears about her appearance, by no means allayed as he sauntered towards her, eyeing her with amusement.

'Fun and games?' he wanted to know gently.

'Bedtime,' she informed him succinctly. 'We don't reckon to look glamorous at this time of day. We're lucky if we get to supper in one piece.' She thrust in a hairpin with an impatient hand. 'Did you want to see someone?'

'You.'

She sternly curbed the tide of pleasure rising beneath her grubby apron. 'Oh? Well, it's not very easy, you can see that, can't you? And there are only two of us. Is it something you could say while I finish getting Piet into his pyjamas?' She was struck by a sudden and unpleasant thought. 'Do you want to tell me off about something?'

His eyes narrowed with laughter. 'I—tell you off? Why should I want to do that? By all means do whatever you need to do to Piet. You have a day off tomorrow, I believe. Paul has a holiday from school; I thought we might all go to the beach and swim—you do swim?'

She nodded, starry-eyed. 'Nothing spectacular, but I can keep myself from drowning. I'd love to come, but will Paul—that is, won't it spoil his day if I'm there?'

He looked surprised. 'I don't imagine so.

Besides, you two girls can be company for each other if Paul and I want to go off together.'

'Yes, of course,' said Phoebe faintly. The idea of spending a day in Maureen's company didn't please her at all; on the other hand, she might find out more about her—and the doctor, and besides, this time Paul might be more friendly. She stared ahead of her, her sapphire eyes seeing nothing—her swimsuits were both rather dishy, and there was that nice towelling beach smock she hadn't intended to buy and had.

'You're not listening,' said Doctor van Someren, and Phoebe jumped guiltily.

'I beg your pardon—I was just. . . What did you say?'

'Ten o'clock, outside the entrance, and mind you're ready.' His voice changed and became businesslike, a little remote. 'And now I should like to take another look at that admission— Johanna—she's in the end ward, I take it.'

There wasn't much of the evening left by the time Phoebe had had supper. She washed her hair and changed her mind half a dozen times over what she should wear in the morning and then, too restless to go to bed, wrote a long letter home, touching lightly on the episode in Juffrouw Leen's house and not mentioning at all that she was to spend the day with Doctor van Someren on the morrow.

# CHAPTER FIVE

DOCTOR VAN SOMEREN wasted no time in getting to Noordwijk-aan-Zee, and a good thing too, thought Phoebe, for when she had arrived at the hospital entrance at exactly ten o'clock it was to find the doctor at the wheel of the Jaguar with Paul beside him and Maureen, looking a perfect vision in a scarlet and white beach outfit which immediately made Phoebe feel dowdy. Sustaining a polite conversation with her companion on the back seat, even for so short a time, hardly improved her frame of mind. By the time they had arrived, parked the car in the grounds of the Hotel Rembrandt overlooking the sea, and had strolled to the beach, she was beginning to wish that she hadn't come—a wish which weakened under the spell of warm sunlight, a wide blue sky, a wide beach stretching away on either side of her and the inviting sea. They more than offset the doctor's coolly casual manner, Paul's bright stare and Maureen's sugary manner.

The doctor owned one of the gay little chalets set out where the dunes and the sand met, and the two girls went at once to change in the curtained alcove in its well-furnished interior. They emerged presently, in an atmosphere of artificial bonhomie, Maureen drawing all eyes in her scarlet bikini and white cap. It was some consolation to Phoebe that the doctor merely glanced at Maureen without much interest. He did the same to her, too, which she found disappointing, for while she made no effort to compete with her companion, she was aware that she made a pleasant enough picture in her sky-blue swim-suit. She wandered on down to the water's edge, leaving Maureen to wait for Paul and Lucius; the girl was obviously back in favour after whatever it was that had gone wrong when they had called at his house. Phoebe wandered slowly into the chilly water, wondering just how firmly entrenched the governess was in the doctor's household; she seemed full of confidence and very self-assured; he must like her very much, and although she hated to acknowledge it, probably he fancied her as well. She sighed and started to swim seawards.

She was a competent swimmer, no more. Within a few minutes she was overtaken by the other three, cleaving their various ways out to sea with an ease she frankly envied. The doctor had shouted something to her as he passed, but she hadn't heard what he had said and it didn't really matter. She called back brightly and swallowed so much water that she was forced to tread water while she coughed and spluttered. When she had her breath back she turned prudently for the shore; she had come quite a long way—too far, perhaps. She deliberately made her strokes slow and steady—she wasn't tired, only a little scared. All the same, her relief was very real when Lucius idled up beside her.

'Tired?' he asked.

'No—but I've not been quite as far as this before and I'm not sure how far I can go.'

He headed her off so that she found herself swimming parallel with the shore instead of towards it. 'In that case, we can stay as we are,' he told her, 'tell me if you get tired, I'll give you a hand.'

She applied herself to her swimming, happy that he had sought her company, sorry that it took up so much of her attention that she had little opportunity of doing anything else. All the same when he asked: 'Your plans are made for your trip home?' she was able to say: 'Yes, thank you—after my night duty—you remember?' She spoke cautiously, not quite happy about holding conversations in the North Sea while swimming.

She heard him grunt. 'You will fly?'

'Yes, in the morning—I shall be home during the afternoon.'

'You will meet all your friends?'

It was a question. 'Yes.'

'You have a great many. One in particular?'

She thought of Jack and hesitated. 'Not really. You asked me the other day.'

'I forget,' he said laconically, and then: 'Race you in!' and he allowed her to win.

They were lying on the sand, soaking up the sun, when Maureen and Paul joined them and Lucius asked the boy to go to the chalet and fetch the flask of coffee they had brought with them, but it was Maureen who suggested with an air of great friendliness that Phoebe might like to go with him. 'For he'll never manage the mugs as well,' she said gaily. As Phoebe got to her feet she watched the little smile on Maureen's face. It was amused and faintly contemptuous and she made no effort to hide it because Lucius was lying on his back with his eyes shut, and there was no need.

In the chalet they found the coffee and a tin of biscuits, and when Phoebe asked Paul where she should find the mugs, he shrugged his shoulders and turned his back, making for the door.

'There's no need to be rude,' she told him firmly. 'I asked a civil question and I deserve a civil answer.'

He shrugged his shoulders again and pointed to a wall cupboard. 'They're there.'

She collected four, added spoons and asked: 'Paul, why do you dislike me?'

He stuck out his lower lip. 'I don't know you,' he muttered.

'No—and I don't know you, do I? But that's no reason to dislike a person.'

He gave her a flickering glance from his dark eyes. 'Maureen says you're. . .' He stopped, and she saw that he wasn't going to say anything more, but at least she had a clue. Heaven knew what the girl had told him. She said quietly: 'Let's go, shall we?'

They lunched at the hotel and later bathed again, but this time Lucius didn't come near her in the water, and yet he had been his usual kindly self at lunch and a very attentive host. She swam around for a little while, then went and lay on the sand waiting for the others, wondering when they would go back—after tea, she supposed, a meal which they took picnic fashion from a tray brought out from the hotel. It was still warm. Phoebe would have liked to have stayed where she was, soaking up the sun and dreaming, but instead she was forced to keep alert, answering Maureen's sly questions and parrying her remarks, sweetly made. 'Such a pity you don't have more time to swim—you poor thing, having to work so hard, you never have a chance to get good at anything, do you?' Her voice dripped kindness.

'No,' said Phoebe, her voice pleasant although she seethed, 'but it wouldn't make any difference. I'm far too cowardly.'

'Oh, never that! Cautious, perhaps—some people have no spirit of adventure. . .'

Phoebe had thought Lucius to be asleep, he had been so quiet, but now he interrupted them. 'A remark which can hardly be applied to Phoebe. I doubt if she would have come to Holland otherwise.' He rolled over and looked at her and smiled lazily. 'You'll come back to dinner, Phoebe? It will be a pleasant end to a pleasant day.'

She thanked him nicely. Only his innate kindness and his beautiful manners had made him invite her, she felt sure, but the invitation gave her a badly needed uplift. 'I've only got my beach clothes with me,' she told him.

His unexpected: 'I like blue, it suits you,' took

her quite by surprise and he went on: 'I'm sure none of us mind, and it will give me a good excuse to wear a shirt and slacks.'

He kept his word. When Phoebe went downstairs after making the best of her appearance in one of the beautiful bedrooms at the back of the house, it was to find him as informally dressed as she was so that she forgot the blue and white cotton shift she was wearing—forgot it until Maureen joined them. She, clever girl, had changed into an artlessly simple white dress which showed off her tan to perfection and made her look like some Greek goddess. She had brushed her dark hair until it gleamed and wore plain gold hoops as earrings, and on her bare feet she had gold kid sandals—she was wearing false eyelashes too, and Phoebe drew a thin trickle of comfort from the knowledge that her own, long and curling, were more than their equal. Secure in this knowledge, she was able to compliment Maureen upon her appearance in a serene manner before going to sit by Paul, whom she engaged in uneasy conversation until dinner was ready.

Because Paul was to dine with them, the meal had been put forward half an hour and they ate it in a room at the back of the house, filled with mellow old furniture, the table decked with fine china and silver worn paper-thin with age. The talk was general, and because Paul was with them, of a lighthearted nature. Phoebe, despite the presence of Maureen, enjoyed herself even though the boy avoided speaking to her and his

governess, in a dozen subtle ways, allowed her
to see just how firmly she was entrenced in the
doctor's household. But Lucius at least made it
his business to entertain her, so that her chagrin
was all the more intense when, after dinner and
when Paul had gone to bed, she suggested that
she should go back to hospital and Lucius made
no attempt to persuade her to stay, as he might
well have done, for it was still early.

'I'll run you back,' he told her, and got to his
feet with no sign of regret, and when she protested that she could walk the short distance, he
took no notice at all but walked with her to the
door while she bade Maureen good night.

They were halted at the door by that young
lady's: 'Don't be long, will you, Lucius, and will
you take me home? All that fresh air has made
me too sleepy to be sociable tonight.'

Lucius had nodded without speaking and
Phoebe got into the car beside him wondering
what exactly Maureen had meant—was she in
the habit of keeping him company in the
evenings, or was she merely once more
reminding Phoebe that she was firmly
entrenched both in the doctor's home and his
affections? She mulled it over while they drove
to the hospital in silence. It was only when he
stopped before its entrance that he spoke.

'I enjoyed our day. Perhaps we may do it
again, Phoebe. I hope you enjoyed it too, though
perhaps not as much as I.' He turned to look at
her. 'I'm indebted to your sister for persuading

you to take her place—we might never have met.'

Phoebe sought for a suitable answer to this and could think of none. After a short silence, she came up with: 'I enjoyed myself very much, thank you, Doctor. . .'

'Lucius.'

'Lucius.' She smiled at him. 'Good night.'

For answer he bent his head to kiss her, a gentle kiss on the corner of her mouth. 'I've been meaning to do that for some time,' he informed her, 'but I've such an infernal bad memory!' He got out of the car, opened her door and waited by it until the porter had opened the wicket in the door. She looked back and waved a little uncertainly and he raised a hand in casual salute. All the way over to the Home she was wondering if he was going to kiss Maureen good night too.

She woke the next morning to the realisation that she would be going on night duty that evening and she didn't particularly want to. It would mean that she wouldn't see anything of Lucius; consultants didn't do rounds at night, they had their registrars and housemen for that. Only upon very rare occasions or in some emergency did they appear on the wards, and that wasn't very often. She would have to resign herself to not seeing him at all and the idea didn't please her at all. She told herself what fun it had been trying to capture his attention; that it had been amusing even if not very successful, but at least he had noticed her a little and the detestable Maureen hadn't liked it. Presumably the doctor was old and wise enough to know what he was about, but Phoebe distrusted the governess as well as disliking her, nor did she think that she had a good influence upon Paul, despite her air of efficiency.

She wished she knew more about the fracas in his house, too, although Maureen had got back into his good graces quickly enough, surely a sign that he fancied her, for he had been very angry. . . Phoebe reminded herself that she was very sorry for him. She frowned at her reflection as she pinned on her cap and repeated, out loud, that she was sorry for him for all the world as though she had contradicted herself. He was wrapped up in his work, unnoticing of the web Maureen was spinning for him—and Paul, would she be good to him? She thought not, for she wasn't the maternal type and the little boy badly needed mothering. She went down to breakfast and consumed her coffee and *boterham*, her head full of gloomy thoughts, not the least of which was that, counting her nights off, it would be a full two weeks before she would see Lucius again.

She was mistaken, for, coming off duty the next morning, yawning her head off and longing for her bed, she found him waiting at the head of the basement stairs.

'Five minutes,' he told her without preamble, and when she looked at him, bewildered. 'You'd better have a cup of coffee, we can breakfast after our swim.'

'Our swim?' she repeated stupidly, her eyes huge for want of sleep. 'Is this something you forgot to tell me, Doctor van Someren?'

He looked thoughtful. 'Possibly—you know what a head I have for remembering things, you must make allowances—anyway, I've told you now, haven't I?'

'I'm tired.'

'So am I,' he assured her. 'I've been up half the night. We need some exercise, so bustle up like a good girl. I'll be in the car.'

It was ridiculous, she told herself, half laughing, half angry, as she tore off her uniform and flung on a cotton dress, pulled the pins out of her hair, brushed it perfunctorily, tied it back anyhow and raced downstairs, her swimsuit under her arm.

'Honestly,' she declared roundly as Lucius opened the Jaguar's door, 'I've not had time to do anything—I look a sight!'

'For sore eyes. Is that not what you say? You should wear your hair like that more often.'

'In a tangle?' she asked incredulously, 'and with nothing on my face—I feel awful.'

He was going slowly through the still quiet streets of Delft. 'At least you do not have to waste time putting on your eyelashes,' he observed mildly. 'Now shut your eyes and take a nap, I'll wake you when we get to Noordwijk.'

It was difficult to open her eyes; Phoebe felt his hand on her shoulder, but the urge to ignore it was very strong, but the hand was gently persistent, she woke up and found that he had parked the car in the hotel grounds again. 'Come on, lazybones,' he teased her gently as he helped her out of the car, put a key into her hand and said: 'Get undressed while I order breakfast,' and strolled away.

Once she had shaken off sleep she felt better, and by the time she was in her swimsuit she felt almost normal again. It was a lovely morning, cool enough to make her shiver a little as she came out of the chalet to find Lucius waiting for her.

She went to the water's edge, her toes curling under the chilly little waves, poking her hair unceremoniously into her cap, and he joined her there. She had barely tucked the last few stray curls away when he caught her briskly by the hand and ran her into the sea. The water was cold but not unkindly so. Phoebe gasped and laughed and finally swam, feeling her body glow and an energy she didn't know she possessed after a hard night's work.

'This is gorgeous—I could go on for ever!'

He made a wide circle round her, tearing through the water at a great rate before settling alongside her. 'You see? I knew you would feel better for it. We'll do this every morning while you're on night duty.'

He gave her a gentle shove in the direction of the beach.

'But your time?'

'There's always time to do the things one wishes to do, have you not discovered that?' He rolled over on to his back, paddling along slowly to keep pace with her earnest efforts. 'I don't start work until nine or half past, and we shall be back by then.'

'But Paul—won't you miss seeing him off to school?' she spluttered, her mouth full of water. 'And won't he mind!' she managed.

'We go our own ways in the morning—in the winter we breakfast together and during his holidays, of course. When he was quite a little boy we agreed about certain things. He understands that not having a mother he must accept that some things have to be different.'

Something in his voice warned her not to ask any more questions. When they reached the beach she said lightly: 'That was really marvellous—and how lovely it is with almost no one here.'

His eyes swept the empty expanse of sand. 'Just the two of us,' he agreed, and his eyes came to rest on hers. 'Lovely.' And something in his face made Phoebe say hastily, 'I'll go and change, I won't be a minute.'

They ate a gargantuan breakfast, sharing the hotel's large dining room with only a handful of people, for it was not yet nine o'clock. Phoebe, buttering toast with a lavish hand, observed: 'I could stay up all day, I feel so wide awake,' and had the remark greeted by a derisive chuckle from her companion.

'I'll check on that tomorrow morning,' he promised her, 'and now if you've finished. . .?'

An hour later, sitting up in bed, she felt so full of energy still that she decided that she wouldn't sleep; she would read for an hour or so and then get up and make a cup of tea. But she didn't open her book at once. She was wondering what Maureen would think, and possibly say, when she discovered that Lucius had taken her swimming and that the exercise was going to be repeated each morning until she went to England. Her satisfaction at the thought of Maureen's annoyance was tinged by regret at having to leave Delft, even for a few days. It would be lovely to see Sybil married, but she wished it could have been at some other time. She closed her eyes on the thought and slept.

She didn't wake until she was called at half past six and when she told Lucius that in the morning they laughed about it together. By the third morning she managed to have a cup of coffee on the ward, so as not to keep him waiting while she went to the dining room, and when they returned from their swim she changed into her cotton dress and sandals, put up her hair and went out to buy another beach outfit. She was coming out of the shop, a woefully expensive but eminently becoming ensemble dangling in its gay carrier bag, when she met Maureen—the last person she wished to see, for she was longing for her bed. The fine energy engendered by her swim was oozing slowly away and she was in no state to parry Maureen's clever thrusts, and she wasn't sure if her temper, now she was tired, would stand up to pinpricks. Maureen had stopped, so Phoebe braced herself.

But there was no need. The governess was

pleasant, even friendly—she mentioned the early morning swim and gave her opinion that it was a splendid idea; she sympathised about the lack of time Phoebe had in which to enjoy herself while she was on night duty too. 'But you'll make up for that at your sister's wedding, won't you?' she suggested, laughing.

Phoebe tried to clear her sleep-laden wits. Maureen was behaving quite out of character and she wondered why. Besides, she was sure that she had never mentioned her trip to England to her. 'I didn't know I had told you,' she essayed.

'Oh, you didn't,' her companion agreed, 'but of course Lucius tells me everything—naturally.' Her dark eyes rested upon Phoebe's own blue sleepy ones. 'I know a great deal about you,' she laughed with a merriment which struck a discordant note in Phoebe's ear, 'so I shouldn't confide in Lucius if you want to keep any secrets from me.'

'I haven't any secrets,' said Phoebe flatly, then went a little pink. She certainly didn't want Maureen to know that she had taken Sybil's place, but surely Lucius. . .

The girl before her broke into her thoughts. 'No? Then you must be a paragon—I've got dozens.' Her glance slid to the package Phoebe was carrying. 'Shopping? It's a waste of time, my dear. Haven't you discovered that he doesn't notice—at least, not unless he's interested in the girl wearing them. Well, I must be off. 'Bye.'

Phoebe, despite her weariness, went over the

conversation word by word before she finally went to sleep and decided that Maureen had wanted to make certain that she didn't trespass on her preserve—Lucius van Someren. 'And I wouldn't,' said Phoebe sleepily, 'if I were sure she loved him, but she doesn't.'

There was a message the next morning to say that Lucius wouldn't be able to take her swimming and just for a moment she wondered if it was Maureen's doing, but she didn't think Lucius would allow anyone to dictate to him about what he should do and what he shouldn't. And anyway, there was no sense in brooding over it. She accepted an invitation from two of the nurses to go with them and have coffee in the city and look at the shops, an occupation which filled the morning hours very satisfactorily and made her so tired that she fell asleep the moment her head touched the pillow.

She knew, the moment she opened the ward door that evening, that it was going to be a bad night—Zuster Witsma looked worried for a start, which was so unlike her that there had to be something wrong, and far too many children were wailing and calling out for attention, which was so unlike their usual sleepy high jinks that Phoebe asked at once:

'What's hit us?' and then remembered that Mies might not quite understand, for her English, though fluent, was strictly textbook. 'They're unhappy,' she substituted, and the Dutch girl said worriedly:

'Oh, Phoebe, such a day—and a nurse off

sick. An infection, how do you say?'

'Bug,' supplied Phoebe unthinkingly.

'Bug? I thought that a bug was an insect.' Mies frowned because she was a stickler for getting her words right.

'It is, but it's what we call a virus infection—any infection—it's slang.'

'Ah,' Mies smiled faintly, 'now I have a new word. There is a bug of the alimentary tract. . .'

'D and V,' interposed Phoebe, and explained rapidly what it was.

'Exactly so—so horrid for the children and no rest for any of us all day. I'm afraid you will have a busy night, you and Zuster Pets—you will find gowns to wear in the treatment room and they are all on Mist. Kaolin and some of the worst are on Phenergan. Doctor van Someren thinks that it is not serious—twenty-four hours, perhaps a little longer. It plays havoc with the diets.'

Phoebe put down her cloak and bag, preparatory to taking the report, as Zuster Pets came into the office—a nice girl, large and rather slow but very patient and thorough. Phoebe and she exchanged a friendly hello and Phoebe thought how funny it was that a junior student nurse should be addressed as Zuster while she herself was called Nurse—an interesting point to take up with Lucius when next she saw him. Probably she wouldn't see him—she wrenched her mind away from that possibility and gave her attention to Zuster Witsma, painstakingly reading the

report in both Dutch and English for the benefit
of both of them.

She had been right about them being busy; it
was almost midnight before the majority of the
children, worn out and washed out, dropped off
to sleep; only a handful of them remained awake,
wretchedly ill and disposed to make the most of
it. Phoebe went soft-footed up and down the
wards, from bed to cot and back to bed again,
feeling sorry for their occupants, for they were
already fighting one disease, it was too bad that
they had to endure this setback as well. Doctor
Pontier had been in earlier in the evening,
expressed satisfaction as to the small patients'
conditions, amended some of the charts, drunk
a hasty cup of coffee, invited Phoebe to go out
to dinner with him when she returned from
England, and went away with the earnest request
that she should call him if she found it necessary.

He had barely closed the doors behind him
when Night Sister arrived to do her round. She
was a short, frankly outsize body, adored by
the nurses. She had twinkling blue eyes, several
chins, and had buried two husbands, and
although she had none of her own she understood
and liked children. Walking with a surprising
lightness despite her ample proportions, she
went from one child to the next, nodded her head
in satisfaction and made her silent way from the
ward, warning Phoebe to send Zuster Smit to her
midnight meal, but on no account to leave the
ward herself.

Alone in the ward, and all the children

miraculously asleep, Phoebe settled down at the desk—they wouldn't stay quiet all night, but she had a short respite in which to chart temperatures and note the medicines she had given. She had done the first three or four when she became aware of footsteps on the stairs—unhurried and quiet—and she knew whose they were; she looked over her shoulder and Lucius was standing just inside the door.

Phoebe got up with the faintest of rustles from her gown and waited for him to reach the desk. He had been out, for he was in a dinner jacket, her imagination, always lively, pictured Maureen waiting outside in his car, looking glamorous, while she— She glanced down at the voluminous folds of thick white cotton while she schooled her delightful features into a look of calm enquiry.

His voice was very quiet. 'Good evening, Nurse Brook—I'm glad to see that they've settled. They had us all a little worried today—were they very troublesome?'

She spoke calmly, in a voice as soft as his. 'Oh, yes, very, but wouldn't we all be? They're worn out.'

He laughed soundlessly. 'And you?'

She gave him an austere look. 'Not in the least. Besides, I have Zuster Pets on with me, and she's a gem of a nurse.'

He looked interested. 'Is she now? We must keep an eye on her, since you say that.'

'For heaven's sake,' she uttered, 'that's only what I think...sir.'

'But I value your opinion, Phoebe, even when you call me sir in that repressive fashion.'

'I'm on duty,' she reminded him.

'Yes—unfortunately,' and when she gave him a questioning look: 'I'd like to take a look at Wil—and Jantje was a little off colour too.'

He took off his jacket and she tied him into a gown and went with him as he went to look at the children. When he had finished and was putting on his jacket again, he said very quietly: 'It's peaceful now—but it can't last all night. I don't envy you, even with the redoubtable Pets to be your right hand.' He smiled suddenly. 'Shall I stay and keep you company until she comes back, Phoebe?'

She couldn't see his face clearly in the dimness of the ward. She handed him a chart to initial and said in a steady, practical voice:

'You'll need to go to bed, you must have had a hard day.'

'A polite brush-off!' He sounded as though he were laughing.

'Oh, I didn't mean it to be,' she whispered anxiously. 'I'd love you to. . .' she stopped herself. 'I have a great deal of work to do,' she informed him sedately.

He nodded. 'A quarter to eight tomorrow morning,' he invited her. 'As it's Saturday, Paul will be coming too.'

'That will be nice, thank you,' and then, because she was unable to prevent herself, 'and Maureen?'

Lucius looked surprised. 'No—she doesn't

live with us, you know. I have no idea at what time she gets up, but I imagine early rising isn't one of her strong points. She prefers her amusements to take place in the evening.'

He was standing very close to her; he had bent his head and kissed her and was at the door, his quiet, 'Good night, Phoebe,' a faint echoing whisper, before she moved.

She was a little late off duty in the morning and tired and faintly ill-tempered with it, but this feeling melted miraculously away as she got to the hospital entrance and saw the Jaguar standing waiting. It disappeared completely as Lucius opened the door for her and squeezed her in beside them, saying: 'You've had a wretched night, haven't you? Do you want to talk about it? I promise you I won't be bored, and Paul won't either.'

She smiled at the boy as the doctor started the car. 'Why, are you going to be a doctor too, Paul?'

He forgot to scowl, his face lighted with interest. 'I'm going to be a vet.'

'Oh, splendid,' said Phoebe with enthusiasm. 'I've an uncle who's a vet. I used to stay with him when I was a little girl; he let me help him, though I suppose I was never much use. Will you go to a veterinary college in Holland?'

He explained at great length and in great detail, and by the time they arrived on the beach, Phoebe thought that he had got over his dislike of her, but somehow, at some time, something went wrong to make him dislike her again, for in the middle of a laughing conversation with Lucius she looked up to find the boy's eyes fixed upon her with such suspicion and animosity that she was completely taken aback, lost the thread of what she was saying, and had to make some excuse for doing so, and although she continued to laugh and talk as before, the morning, for her at any rate, was spoilt. Her spirits were hardly improved by the doctor's careless statement that he would be going to Vienna for several days on the morrow, 'by which time you will be in England,' he reminded her cheerfully. 'And by the way, young van Loon will drive you to the airport,' and when she protested, he declared: 'He's been waiting to take you out ever since he met you. This will be the next best thing—he's a nice boy,' and his last remark capped her unsatisfactory morning: 'A little young for you, though.'

Tiredness and some feeling she didn't bother to analyse dissolved into a little spurt of temper. 'In that case, perhaps you'd better warn him not to go with me—there must be some middle-aged taxi-driver whom you might consider more suitable. I had planned to go by train.'

He had either not noticed her pettishness or chose to ignore it.

'Oh, lord, a ghastly journey—that's why I suggested to van Loon that he might take you. Much better go with him, Phoebe. Besides, he'll be so disappointed if you don't—you know what these young men are.'

'Do I?' Her voice was glacial.

He stopped the car outside the hospital and turned to look at her.

'I imagine that you have dealt kindly with dozens of them.' He smiled with such charm that Phoebe found herself smiling back.

'If you're warning me not to gobble him up, I won't,' she assured him, and turned to say goodbye to Paul, sitting in the back of the car, and although he answered politely enough she could see that he disliked her still. She sighed a little, thanked the doctor for her trip, wished him a pleasant stay in Vienna, and got out of the car. She turned to wave before she went into the hospital, but they had already gone.

She felt lonely during the next few days; she told herself it was because she was tired from her night duty, and even though she went out each morning with one or other of the nurses, the days lagged sadly. It was a relief when she had gone on duty for the last time, packed her case and gone downstairs to meet young Doctor van Loon. At least he was delighted to see her, and made no secret of his admiration. Although she was tired and unaccountably despondent, she found herself enjoying the drive to Schipol; they parted like old friends when her flight was called and she left him vowing that he should take her out for the day when she returned.

The journey passed swiftly, for she had been up all night and slept a good deal, and when she wasn't sleeping, her mind was far too weary to allow her to think coherently, but at Shaftesbury,

when she got out of the train and found Sybil and
Nick waiting for her, her tiredness evaporated in
the spate of news—the wedding, on the day after
next, naturally took pride of place, and it wasn't
until they were home, sitting round the table
eating the belated tea Aunt Martha had prepared,
that Sybil asked:

'Well, Phoebe, how's the scheme going? Is it
fun? Do you see much of the doctor and has
he noticed you yet?' She laughed and Phoebe
laughed with her, aware, to her annoyance, that
her cheeks had turned a good deal pinker
than usual.

'The scheme's fine,' she replied hastily. 'I
love working there—the Ward Sister's about my
age and we're good friends. Doctor van Someren
comes each day, sometimes more often. He's
nice.' As she said it she knew what an understate-
ment that was, but for some reason she didn't
want to talk about him; but the others did.

'And is he married?' Nick wanted to know,
and Sybil chimed in. 'Yes, you said precious
little about him in your letters.'

'Well—' began Phoebe, and went on hastily:
'No, he's not, but he's got an adopted son, Paul.
He's almost nine and rather a dear, only he
doesn't like me.'

'Why ever not?' asked Sybil. 'How funny—
but you must have seen quite a lot of him, then.'

Phoebe made quite a business of buttering a
scone. 'No, not really. I met him and then I went
to the doctor's house with Zuster Witsma after
we went to the botanical garden at Leyden...'

'Who took you?'

She evaded her sister's eye. 'It was something I was supposed to see—part of the scheme. . .'

'Who took you?' Sybil was nothing if not persistent.

'I went with Zuster Witsma—Doctor van Someren took me round.'

'Did he talk?'

'Yes, of course. He's a perfectly ordinary man.' She paused for a moment; he wasn't ordinary in the least, he was someone quite different. Phoebe dragged her attention back to what she was saying. 'We saw the museum too, it was very interesting.'

'What did he talk about?'

'Oh, the garden and plants and the hospital.' She looked down at her plate, remembering all the other things he had said.

'Charming—he sounds a bit dreary.'

'He's not,' said Phoebe sharply. 'He's a. . .' She stopped, not wanting to put her shadowy thought into words. 'I say, I've brought your wedding present with me, would you like to see it?'—a successful digression which sent everybody up to her room while she unpacked the Delftware coffee set and offered it to the happy pair.

She went to bed early, finding it pleasant to be in her own room again, so quiet and peaceful after the bustle of Delft and the noise from the wards. She went to sleep at once, but not before she had thought about Lucius and wondered where he was and what he was doing. It was too much to hope that he might miss her as she undoubtedly missed him. She slept on that not very happy thought.

There was too much to do the next day for anyone to have time to ask her any more questions. The wedding wasn't to be a large one, but even though they hadn't many relations, they had a great many friends, and Nick's family was a large one. They all drove over to Shaftesbury that evening, where his parents were staying for a couple of days. There were a round dozen for dinner and a very light-hearted meal it was, only broken up by Aunt Martha's firm decision that the bride required her beauty sleep.

Phoebe, waking early the next morning, went at once to her window. The weather had been unbelievably fine for weeks, and if it were to rain it would mean a last-minute rearranging of the buffet lunch which they were to have in the garden behind the house. But she need not have worried. The pale morning sky was clear and the sun, already bright, shone on to flower beds which really looked at their best. The roses were out too; the first buds of the Lady Seton had opened overnight, their pink the exact colour of the dress Phoebe had chosen to wear. She had a wide straw hat to go with it too, laden with matching roses—it was a beautiful hat and she looked nice in it. She found herself wishing that Doctor van Someren were there to see her in it.

She withdrew her head from the window, frowning a little. She was becoming obsessed by the man! She really must try to remember that however interesting she might find him, she wasn't likely to see him once she had left Delft, and that would be soon enough, she remembered with something like a shock as she went downstairs to the kitchen to make the morning tea.

The wedding went off brilliantly and was all that such an event should be. After it was all over and the bride and groom had left, the last of the guests gone and Aunt Martha had retired to her room, happy but worn out, Phoebe went into the garden and sat down in the still bright evening. It had been a wonderful day. Sybil had looked lovely and so very happy and everything had gone without a hitch—besides, it had been fun to meet old friends again, only she hadn't expected to see Jack there. She wondered who had invited him and then dismissed the thought as not worth bothering about. He had greeted her with an assurance which had annoyed her, as though he had only to raise his finger and she would come running.

She moved a little on the bench under the tree, smoothing the silk of her dress with careful fingers; it wasn't until she had come face to face with Jack that she had known that she really didn't care if she never saw him again. There was only one person she wanted to see—Lucius van Someren. She supposed, now that she allowed herself to think about it, that she had been in love with him all the time, only she hadn't been prepared to admit it. She sighed and got up and strolled down a garden path and, careless of her fine dress, leaned over the low stone wall at its end. There was Maureen to consider—it was impossible to tell from Lucius' manner what he felt about the girl, and as for herself, he had shown nothing but a pleasant friendliness towards her. And the dice were loaded against her, for Paul hated her and he and Maureen were a formidable barrier between her and the doctor. She felt helpless and hopeless out there in the darkening garden. The only thing which buoyed her up was the fact that she would be seeing him again in a couple of days.

She started walking back to the house, telling herself with a certain amount of force that one never knew what lay around the corner.

# CHAPTER SIX

As it happened, it was Doctor Pontier round the corner. He was waiting for Phoebe at Schipol, and she, who had passed the flight in an indulging of impossible daydreams in which Lucius had come to meet her with every sign of delight, had difficulty in schooling her face into an expression of pleased surprise at the sight of his registrar.

He took her case and walked her out to where his car stood waiting.

'The boss asked van Loon to pick you up,' he explained, 'but I tossed him for it.' He laughed and Phoebe, of necessity, laughed with him.

'What about the ward round?' she asked.

'Jan will stand in for me. I told the boss—he said it didn't matter to him who fetched you as long as someone did.'

She was aware of ruffled feelings. It was rather like being a parcel which had to be collected; so much for her half-formed plans and hopes! She had allowed herself to drift from one delightful dream to the next during the last couple of days, and a lot of good they were doing her—a little realism would be a good thing. She turned to her companion and said cheerfully: 'Well, it's jolly nice to see you. I was just a bit worried about getting to Delft, though I'm sure it's easy enough—but this is much nicer. I wonder when I'm expected on duty?'

He got into the car and started the engine. 'I rather think this afternoon—there's a staff nurse off sick, nothing much, but she could be cooking up something. Mies will be glad to see you.'

Nice to be wanted, thought Phoebe, nice to fill a niche, even a humble one. Even nicer if Lucius wanted her back too. She resolutely put him out of her mind and entertained Doctor Pontier with some of the lighter aspects of Sybil's wedding.

She didn't see Lucius until the evening, when after a heavy afternoon's work, he came quietly on to the ward, Mies and Arie with him. She had already seen these two, of course, but there had been little time to say much, only Mies had found time to apologise for asking Phoebe to go straight on duty. She smiled at Phoebe as they came down the ward now, but it was Doctor van Someren who spoke, and his impersonal friendliness chilled the warmth she felt at seeing him again.

'Nurse Brook, we are more than glad to see you back again. I hope you had a pleasant time at your sister's wedding? You were fortunate to have such splendid weather.'

She murmured something unintelligible to this rather prosy remark, but as he wasn't listening she might just as well have said nothing at all. 'Wil,' he went on immediately, 'I'm not too happy about the child. We changed the dosage, didn't we? But the chest infection doesn't respond—we had better try something else.' He turned to Arie Lagemaat and switched to Dutch, and Phoebe, called by one of the children, went to attend to his small wants. When she had finished, Lucius had gone.

She met Paul the next day. The weather had changed with ferocious suddenness to a grey sky, a fine continuous rain and a high wind, but Phoebe, restless and disappointed at Lucius's lack of interest in her return, decided to go out. There was still a great deal of Delft to see; she hadn't visited the Tetar van Elven Museum yet; she dragged on a raincoat and tied a scarf over her hair without bothering overmuch as to her appearance, and started out. She had hours of time, for she had got up early after a night of wakefulness, and she wasn't on until two o'clock.

She lingered in the museum, drinking the coffee she was offered when she had toured its treasures, and then, because there was no sign of the rain abating, started off once more, walking a little aimlessly, until she remembered that she hadn't had more than a hurried peep at the Oude Delft canal; she would walk its length and fill in the time until she was due back on duty. She was halfway along the street bordering it, when the urge to explore one of the narrow lanes branching from it sent her down the nearest, dim and cobbled and on this wet day, dreary. She had reached the right-angled bend near its end when she heard the running feet behind her. They sounded urgent and Phoebe stopped, glancing to right and left of her, conscious that her heart was beating faster. Probably it was someone taking a short cut in a hurry. But it was Paul, tearing round the corner and stopping short within a foot of her. She managed a calm 'Hullo, Paul,' and waited for him to speak.

When he did, she could hear the excitement in his voice. 'I saw you,' he told her, 'and I wondered if you wanted someone to show you the city.'

She was taken aback. 'That's nice of you, Paul—I've just been to the museum in the Koornmarkt and I've an hour to spare still. I wasn't really going anywhere—and shouldn't you be going home?'

He looked away from her. 'No, I—I came out of school early this morning. I could show you some really old houses, near here.' He sounded eager. 'They're mediaeval and not used any more.'

Phoebe hesitated. She had time to spare, it was true, and this was the first occasion upon which Paul had shown any real signs of wanting to be friends. She said quickly: 'All right—where do we go first?'

For a boy of his age, he knew his home city well. They went up one *steeg* and down the next while he pointed out the interesting points of the buildings surrounding them. At length Phoebe glanced at her watch.

'Heavens,' she exclaimed, 'a quarter of an hour left! I must go.'

'One more,' he begged. 'There's a warehouse

along here, by the canal.' He led the way through
a narrow alley to a cobbled street, a canal on one
side, narrow houses, grey and anonymous with
age, on the other. They were deserted, forlorn in
the rain which pattered into the dark, sluggish
water of the canal.

Phoebe shivered. 'My goodness—this all
looks a bit gloomy! Surely there's nothing. . .'

But Paul had crossed to one of the warehouses
and pushed its door open. 'It's empty,' he told
her. 'I've been inside lots of times. The room on
the top floor is marvellous—you should just
see it.'

Phoebe glanced up at the steep gable above
their heads. It looked a long way away. 'I don't
think I want to,' she said. 'I'll take your word
for it.'

She knew she had said the wrong thing the
moment she finished speaking; he gave her a
look of scorn and said: 'Chicken! I didn't know
you were frightened.'

'I'm not frightened,' she protested vigorously,
'only I don't see the point of climbing all those
stairs. . .'

Paul turned away, his shoulders hunched. He
said coldly: 'You keep saying you want us to be
friends, but you don't really.'

'Is that what you want? Just to prove my
friendship—to climb some stairs and look
at a room?' she asked robustly. 'OK, five
minutes, then.'

He went inside first and although it sounded
empty and hollow, there was nothing unpleasant

about the old house. He led the way rapidly up the creaking stairs to the first floor and then up successively narrow staircases to the landings above, until on the third landing there was only a narrow twisting staircase in the wall, its steps worn and uneven. Paul went first to open the small door at the top—a heavy door, Phoebe could see, with great bolts top and bottom. She went past the boy into the dimness beyond and found an empty room; it smelled musty and close and because the shutter was barred across the window on the outside, it was darker than it need have been. She rotated slowly, staring round her. 'Why,' she cried, 'there's nothing here. . .' and turned her head sharply and too late at the sound of the door shutting. Paul had gone; she listened to the bolts being shot with a kind of stunned surprise, but only for a moment. She ran over to the door and rapped on it.

'Paul—I know you're having a joke, but I really haven't time. Will you open the door? I shall have to run all the way to the hospital!'

His young voice sounded thin through the thick wood. 'It's not a joke—Maureen says you're a scheming woman, out to catch Papa—well, you can't now. You didn't think I could be clever, did you? I knew if I waited I'd catch you!'

Before she could draw astonished breath to reply to this speech, he had gone down the stairs. She could hear his feet, echoing hollowly as he went further and further away. When she heard the bang of the street door she gave up calling after him and leaned against the door, trying to think of a way out. The door was fast enough, and far too thick to yield to a hairpin, even if she knew how to use it—besides, there were the bolts, they would surely need a crowbar. The shuttered window wasn't any good either. Phoebe tried shouting through it, but the glass was thick and set in small leaded panes. She peered at her watch and made out that it was already time for her to be on duty and cheered up a little; very soon someone would wonder where she was, but her heart sank when she remembered that she had told no one where she was going. All she could hope for was that Paul would relent and come back for her, or take fright and tell Lucius—or even Maureen—but would Maureen take the trouble to come and let her out? She thought not. It would have to be Paul, and no doubt when he got home and started to think about it, he would return. Having settled this to her satisfaction, she looked round for somewhere to sit. There was nowhere but the floor, so she took off her raincoat, folded it carefully and sat upon that, her head against the wall. Every ten minutes or so she got up and went to the window and shouted, for surely at some time during the day someone would pass along the street below. She told herself vigorously that of course they would and ignored the fact she and Paul hadn't met a soul. . .

The time passed slowly. Phoebe occupied it by reciting such Dutch words as she had managed to learn, going over the various procedures Lucius favoured for his patients and by writing, in her head, an amusing letter home. Only presently it wasn't amusing; she was hungry and the dry air of the ill-ventilated room had made her thirsty. Besides, the complete stillness of the old house had become something tangible. Supposing it was used by tramps at night, or hippies? After all, Paul had known of it, so others would too... supposing someone came, how was she going to make them understand how she came to be there, locked in? It was a thought she decided not to pursue. She might as well relax and have a nap, she told herself firmly; it was broad daylight, and even if no one knew where to look for her, the police were very good at finding people, so she had absolutely no reason to panic. Probably at this very moment Paul was telling Lucius what he had done. She eased herself on the raincoat, her pretty brow wrinkled. Supposing he didn't— supposing he told Maureen, who appeared to have a strong influence on him, and she decided that they would do nothing about it? After all, it was her ill-chosen words that had put the idea into the boy's head.

Phoebe got up; it was time to shout again. She would, she promised herself, have a heart-to-heart talk with Maureen.

A little hoarse, she settled down again, rehearsing what she would say, and dozed off in the middle of it.

At the hospital, Zuster Witsma had at first been unperturbed at Phoebe's absence. She had gone straight on duty the day before without a word of complaint; probably she had fallen asleep over a book. But when half an hour had passed and there was still no sign of her, she sent over to the Home, only to discover that Phoebe was not to be found and that the hall porter, who had seen her go out that morning, was quite sure she hadn't returned. It seemed a good idea to consult the Directrice, and that good lady was on the ward, conferring with Mies, when Lucius walked on to the ward to collect some papers. The sight of him induced both ladies to tell him about it and the Directrice concluded: 'I find it strange, Doctor van Someren, that Nurse Brook should not return—she is not a young, silly girl even if she is ignorant of our language. I cannot imagine her allowing that to stand in the way of her telephoning or sending a message.' She added firmly: 'I shall try the other hospitals.'

The doctor had said nothing at all—indeed, he appeared so abstracted in his manner that she wondered if he had heard her, but apparently he had, for after a pause he said: 'Yes, do that, Directrice, but please do nothing more until you hear from me. I have an idea—probably I am wide of the mark, but somehow I think not. You will excuse me.'

For a man of such calm and deliberation, his speed as he drove through the Delft streets to his home was excessive. He wasted no time in entering his house either and strode through it to the sitting room where he found Maureen and Paul. The boy had a free afternoon from school; at lunchtime Maureen had assured the doctor that she would take advantage of it and give Paul a lesson in English reading. However, as he entered Paul was sprawled on the floor, playing half-heartedly with a model car, and his governess was stretched out on one of the sofas, deep in a glossy magazine. The doctor frowned as she started up, but when he spoke it was with abrupt courtesy.

'Maureen, I wish to talk to Paul—you will excuse us,' and as she went out of the room he turned to his adopted son.

Paul had got to his feet. He had gone a little white and he looked decidedly guilty—frightened, even. The doctor sighed. His fantastic idea was likely to prove correct, but he had to be sure. With no sign of anger he said:

'Paul, Phoebe hasn't returned to the hospital, and she's more than two hours overdue. I have a hunch that you know where she is. You were scared about something at lunch, weren't you? and you ate nothing to speak of, and when I mentioned that she was back at work you looked— er—shall we say guilty?' He strolled across the room and stood looking out of the window, his back to the little boy. 'I'm right, am I not?'

Paul scuffed his sandals, his eyes on the carpet, and muttered something.

'Yes—well, you shall tell me about it later, but now I want to know where she is.'

He had turned round to face Paul, who shot him a quick look. Something in the doctor's calm voice made him answer immediately.

Lucius left his house without a word. Within seconds he was in his car again, taking short cuts to the old warehouses by the canal. He was still driving much too fast and his face was without expression.

Phoebe had awakened from her brief nap unrefreshed and with a feeling that the room had become smaller, stuffier and very hot while she had slept. She also felt frightened, a sensation she quelled as best she could by going to the window and shouting once again through the shutters; at least it was something to do. She had barely seated herself once more before she was on her feet. There was someone in the house, she had heard the door bang below and now the faint sound of footsteps upon the stairs. She opened her mouth to call out, then almost choked herself with the effort to hold her tongue; if it were someone who knew her, they would surely call to her.

Whoever it was, was coming very fast. She faced the door, scarcely breathing as the bolts were shot back with some force and Lucius walked in. The breath she had been holding escaped in a small sound like a whispered scream mixed in with a sigh of relief. The desire to rush at him and fling herself in his arms was overwhelming, but she suppressed it firmly— and a good thing too, for he looked quite unworried, leaning against the door in a casual fashion, as though he were quite in the habit of releasing those foolish enough to get themselves locked up in deserted warehouses, and thought nothing of it. Her relief was swamped by a splendid rage, so that when he said: 'Hullo, Phoebe—sorry about this,' in a placid voice, her temper was exacerbated so that had there been anything handy to throw at him, she would certainly have thrown it.

Deprived of this method of relieving her pent-up feelings, she said crossly: 'Pray don't mention it, it was hardly your fault.' She looked at him with glittering blue eyes. 'I had a nice sleep,' she informed him, and burst into tears.

His arms were comforting and his shoulder reassuring. Phoebe muttered into the fine cloth of his jacket: 'You could have called out—I-I thought you were a t-tramp or a h-hippy!'

A smile, sternly suppressed, trembled on the doctor's lips although his voice was warmly comforting. 'My poor girl, you must have been terrified. What would you have done?'

'I haven't a clue,' she sobbed.

He spoke softly into her hair. 'I find that hard to believe. You are a woman in a thousand, you would have handled the situation very well, I have no doubt, and probably had them showing you the nearest way to the hospital within minutes.'

She laughed then, and presently, her tears dried, she drew away from him. 'How did you know where I was?'

'Paul told me.'

She glanced at him warily and saw that he was watching her closely. It was most unlikely that the little boy would have told him what he had said to her. She said lightly: 'Aren't little boys awful with their pranks? Don't be hard on him, will you? He was joking—I expect he got scared and didn't know what to do.'

Lucius took a long time to answer. 'Possibly, but even a boy as young as Paul would know that he only had to come back here and let you out.'

She didn't meet his eye. 'Yes—well, thank you very much for coming. I'm afraid I've taken up your precious time.'

'There are things more precious.' He had gone to try the shutters and spoke over his shoulder.

'I'll go back to St Bonifacius at once, I'm hours late.'

'You'll come back with me to my house and have a meal. They were managing very well on the ward, they can continue to do so for another hour.'

Phoebe was shaking out her raincoat. 'I'd rather go back—that is, if you don't mind.'

'I do mind. Besides, Paul is at home, he will want to apologise to you.'

She was flustered and furious with herself for being so—she, who had the reputation of keeping her cool at all times. 'Some other time—it surely doesn't matter. . .'

'Am I to infer that you have some reason for not wishing to meet Paul?' His voice was silky.

'Of course not. Whatever reason should there be?' She put on her raincoat and he crossed the room to help her, turning her round to button it as though she were a little girl.

'A nice cup of tea?' he suggested. 'I know I

need one—I had no idea that I could feel so anxious.'

'About me?' The words had popped out before she could stop them.

'About you.' His hands were on her shoulders and he kept them there. 'I'm responsible for you.'

'So you are,' Phoebe said flatly, feeling elation draining from her. How silly of her to have imagined that his anxiety would have been for any other reason. She said brightly: 'I'm ready. Shall we go?'

Paul and his governess were still in the sitting room, he still on the floor with a book on his knees although he wasn't reading it and she still on the sofa, holding a long glass in one hand and still idly turning the pages of the magazine. She put both glass and magazine down hastily and got to her feet. 'Heavens, how quick you were! We didn't expect you. . . Phoebe, you poor thing! I've been telling Paul what a little horror he is, he should be severely punished.'

Phoebe could sense Lucius' anger, although she wasn't certain against whom it was directed, so before he could speak she said: 'Heavens, why? Didn't you ever play pranks when you were small? I know I did, and what harm's been done? I'm perfectly all right—as a matter of fact, I had a sleep.'

Maureen looked at her narrowly. 'Weren't you the least bit frightened?'

'No,' Phoebe uttered the lie stoutly, 'why should I be in broad daylight? I was a bit worried about getting back on duty, that was all. What was there to be scared about, anyway?'

She avoided the doctor's eye as she spoke, aware that she was gabbling. It was a relief when he spoke, his voice unhurried. 'Maureen, will you be good enough to go and ask Else to make some sandwiches and a pot of tea—Phoebe has missed her lunch.'

She went reluctantly. It wasn't until she had disappeared from the room that he spoke again. 'Paul, will you come here and apologise to Phoebe.'

The boy came and stood before her, giving her a look of mingled appeal and dislike. When he had apologised she said quickly: 'That's all right, Paul. Actually, I enjoyed our morning together, we must do it again some time.' She turned to Lucius. 'Paul's got a marvellous knowledge of Delft and he's a first-rate guide.' She smiled at him, coaxing him to good humour, and was disappointed when his face remained grave. 'I take it that Paul locked you in for a joke?' he asked her.

She felt her cheeks redden. 'Yes, of course,' she spoke quite sharply, 'and I hope that now he's said he's sorry, we needn't say any more about it.'

'You're generous. Very well, we won't. I don't think he'll do such a thing again, will you, Paul?'

The boy shook his head. His sigh of relief sounded loud in the silence which followed the doctor's remark and which was only broken

when Else came in to tell them that she had taken
the tea into the small sitting room at the back of
the hall.

On the surface at least, tea was a pleasant
meal, although Phoebe was the only one to eat
anything. She made thankful inroads into the
sandwiches and Lucius drank his tea—largely,
she felt, to put her at her ease. He talked too,
making sure that they all took their share of the
conversation, keeping to mundane topics so that
any constraint which might still be lurking was
stilled. When she got up to go, Phoebe found
herself more at ease than she had ever felt before
at the house, despite the niggling thought that
there must be some reason for Paul's behaviour
which she hadn't hit upon.

Lucius, it seemed, had to return to hospital
too. They spoke little on the short journey and
in the hospital they parted company, he to go to
the wards, she to the Home. She thanked Lucius
briefly in the hall and was about to turn away
when he dropped a hand on her shoulder to hold
her still.

'Don't disappear again,' he begged her, 'my
nerves won't stand it.'

Phoebe changed with the lightning speed of
long practice and while she anchored her cap,
pondered his remark. Intended as a joke, she
concluded, and indeed, his impersonal friendly
manner towards her when she got on the ward
seemed to bear this out; not that they exchanged
more than a few words, for she was instantly
plunged into the ward work after a brief

explanation to Mies and a slightly longer one to
the Directrice. By the time she had the leisure to
look around her, Lucius had gone.

She didn't see him for several days after
that—they met on the ward, naturally, but never
to speak about anything but ward matters. She
had the impression that he was avoiding her, and
rendered extra sensitive by her love, she made
it easy for him to do so by keeping out of the
way when he did a round and seeing to it that
there was little chance of her being about when
he paid his evening visits. She went out to dinner
with Doctor Pontier, the cinema with Jan, the
houseman, and if that were not sufficient to dis-
tract her interest, accepted an invitation to have
supper with Mies.

Mies had the day off, the Dutch staff nurse
had gone off duty at three o'clock, so Phoebe
found herself in charge of the ward until ten
o'clock—rather a late hour, she had ventured to
point out to Mies, to go out to supper. But Mies
had laughed and told her that she could sleep it
off the next day, as then it would be her day off,
so, while other nurses were getting ready for bed,
Phoebe was wrestling with her hair, changing
her clothes and re-doing her face, rather regret-
ting that she had agreed to go. But Mies was
nice and it would be fun to see her flat. She
snatched up her handbag and raced downstairs
to engage the porter in the difficult task of calling
a taxi for her. He shook his head, however,
smiled and gave her some lengthy explanation
not one word of which could she understand.

She tried again, getting very muddled, and was cut short by Lucius' voice behind her.

'Don't struggle with our abominable language any more, dear girl,' he begged her, half laughing. 'He's only telling you that you don't need a taxi. I'll take you—come along.'

Phoebe stayed just where she was. 'Thank you, but I couldn't possibly give you the trouble. I'm going to Mies, she told me to take a taxi. . .'

He looked conscience-stricken. 'Oh, lord, my memory! I quite intended telling someone or other that I should be calling for you; didn't I?'

He looked at her with raised eyebrows.

'No,' said Phoebe, 'you didn't.'

'I'm going to Mies' flat too.' He added, 'For supper,' as if that clinched the matter.

'Oh, well, are you? It's kind of you!' She petered out, so delighted to be with him for the next hour or so that she was hardly aware of what she was saying. She smiled at the porter, cast a quick, shy look at Lucius and allowed herself to be led out to the Jaguar.

Mies lived close by, down one of the narrow streets leading off a busy main street. The house was old, its ground floor taken up by a bakery, the narrow door beside the shop leading directly on to an equally narrow and steep stairs. The flat was on the top floor, three flights up—two attics, cunningly brought up to date, the mod con tucked away where it couldn't spoil the charm of the old low-ceilinged rooms. Mies had furnished it with bits and pieces, but there were flowers everywhere, highlighting the white walls and the polished wood floor.

Phoebe was whisked away to the bedroom, where Mies exclaimed happily:

'I am so glad that you have come—this is a feast, a celebration, you understand. Arie and I are engaged.'

Phoebe kissed the happy excited face, wished the Dutch girl everything suitable to the occasion and followed her out to the sitting room where there was another round of hand-shaking and kissing, first by Mies and Arie and then by Lucius. For a man of such absent-minded habits, he kissed remarkably well, Phoebe thought confusedly.

'There isn't—that is, it's not me you have to congratulate,' she managed.

His blue eyes were very bright. 'I never lose a good opportunity,' he told her gravely. 'Besides, I also am to be congratulated.'

She studied his face. 'You're going to be married too?' she asked, and managed, with a fair amount of success, to smile at him.

'You are surprised? At the moment it is strictly a secret.' He let her go and went to open the champagne he had brought with him, and the next half hour or so passed in a good deal of lighthearted nonsense and gay talk. Presently, helping Mies fetch in the supper, Phoebe had a few minutes, away from Lucius, to pull herself together—something she achieved to such good effect that she was able, with the help of the champagne and her resolute common sense, to pass the evening in a very credible manner—a little brittle in her talk, perhaps, and her laugh a little too high-pitched, but that was surely better than bursting into tears.

She awoke late, made a sketchy breakfast and decided to go to Amsterdam for the day. It stretched before her, a vista of endless hours until she should see Lucius again. She would have to fill it somehow—just as she would have to fill all the days ahead of her, once she had returned to England. 'The sooner you get him out of your system, my girl,' she told her face as she made it up with care, 'the better.'

She was on her way out of the hospital when she bumped into the youthful van Loon, who said joyfully: 'I say, what luck meeting you like this, Miss Brook. I must bring specimens for Doctor van Someren, but it is also my day off—you will perhaps have coffee with me?'

Any port in a storm. Phoebe gave him a wide smile. 'I'd love to. I was just on my way to catch a train to Amsterdam; I've got a day off too.'

'You're free all day? What luck! May we not go together? I have my car with me. I could show you something of the city.' He grinned widely, 'I would be most happy.'

'What a lovely idea. I'd like that, only we must go Dutch.'

'Go Dutch?' He looked bewildered. 'But I am Dutch.'

Phoebe laughed. 'It's a saying—we use it in English. It means we each pay for ourselves. I won't come otherwise.'

'You do this often in England? This going Dutch?'

'Yes—it's a common practice.' She smiled persuasively. 'No one minds.'

'Then I will not mind also. You will wait here for me?'

He had a Fiat 500, not new; it made the most interesting noises which they occupied themselves in identifying as they drove along. Phoebe, listening to the vague bangings and clangings beneath them, wondered if she would get back safely, but it seemed unsporting to voice her doubts, for her companion was so obviously enjoying himself.

'How long have you had this car?' she wanted to know, and wasn't surprised to hear that he had bought it off another young medic for five hundred guilden, and that this was his first trip of any distance. He added happily that he considered it a lucky coincidence that he should have met her, so that she could enjoy it with him. Phoebe agreed in a hollow voice, her doubts as to whether they would reach Delft again supplanted by the more urgent one as to whether they would reach Amsterdam.

But they did, and what was more, Eddie, as he had begged her to call him, was lucky enough to find a parking place by one of the canals. He stopped the car within inches of the water and oblivious of her shattered nerves, invited her to get out, a request she obeyed with alacrity, to find Lucius watching them from the pavement.

He crossed the road immediately, wished her

a good morning, gave the car a considered stare
and remarked to van Loon: 'I was told you had
bought this car from Muiselaar, but I hardly
credited you with driving it.'

Eddie patted its scratched bonnet with pride.
'It goes like a bomb, sir,' he said simply.

'Yes, I was afraid of that.' Doctor van
Someren made to move away and Phoebe, longing to ask him where he was going, watched him
reach the pavement, only to turn round and come
back again. 'I hope you have a pleasant time,'
he observed. His eyes flickered over van Loon,
whose head was under the boot. 'You will enjoy
being with someone nearer your own age. If by
any chance this—cr— heap should fall apart, be
good enough to telephone the hospital and I will
arrange for someone to collect you.'

He smiled briefly into her surprised face and
once more regained the pavement, to disappear
among the passers-by.

But nothing untoward happened. They spent
a cheerful day together and although it was Eddie
who decided where they should go, it was
Phoebe who kept an eye on the money they spent
and an eye on the clock too.

She treated him like a younger brother—a
relationship which seemed to suit him very
well—and they got on famously. He took her to
the Dam Palace where they wandered round the
state apartments, which Phoebe declared to be
magnificent but dreadfully uncomfortable to live
in; she was whisked across the Dam square to
look at the War Memorial, treading their way

among the hippies to do so, then to drink coffee
at a nearby café and then be walked briskly
through the city's busy streets to the
Rijksmuseum to see the famous Night Watch.
She would have liked a chance to do a little
window-shopping, but Eddie, determined that
she should be stuffed with culture, marched her
remorselessly about the streets, in and out of
museums, standing her on pavements to crane
her pretty neck at the interesting variety of roof-
tops, taking it for granted that she would leap on
and off trams at a word from him. It was fun;
the *broodje met ham* which they stopped to eat
at a snack bar, the rich cream confections they
consumed with their tea during the afternoon,
the postcards she bought to send home—she
thanked him during the drive back—accom-
plished despite the bangs and rattles—refused
his pressing offer to have dinner with him, and
went early to bed, tired out.

She was off duty in the morning, and despite
the drizzling rain, decided to go out. She was at
the hospital entrance when the Jaguar drew up
beside her and Lucius got out. She wished him
a good morning and made to pass him, but he
stopped her with: 'Wait a minute, Phoebe,' and
joined her.

'I've half an hour to spare,' he told her easily.
'I feel like a walk, if you don't mind?' He gave
her a sideways glance. 'You seem determined to
stretch my nerves to breaking point.'

She stopped walking the better to look at him.
'I do? How?'

'That—er—car which van Loon drives is hardly safe. Do tell him when next you go out together that he is to borrow the Mini—he has only to ask.'

'But I don't suppose I shall see him again. . .'

He raised disbelieving eyebrows. 'No? But one day is hardly sufficient in which to see the sights. You had arranged to go with him?'

Phoebe blinked. If she hadn't known the doctor so well she might have deluded herself that he was jealous. 'Of course not! He happened to meet me as I was on my way to catch a train to Amsterdam—he had some specimens of yours to deliver or something of the sort, but he had a day off too—he suggested that I went with him so that he could show me the sights.' She added as an afterthought, 'I didn't know about his car.'

She watched the little smile play around his mouth. 'I was mistaken. It seemed natural that you should spend as much of your free time as possible with someone of your own age.'

'You keep saying that,' she told him, quite put out. 'You know quite well that he's five years younger than I—anyway, I feel old enough to be his mother.'

'Which reminds me—it's Paul's ninth birthday tomorrow, so will you come to tea? You're off in the afternoon, are you not?'

She wondered how he knew that. 'I'd love to. Did he really invite me? I must get him a present. What are you giving him?'

'A wrist watch, but I'm still wondering what

else to buy for him. Have you any suggestions?'

'Mice?'

He laughed. 'An unusual suggestion from a woman—perhaps you like them.'

'I do not, but little boys do—didn't you keep mice?'

'Yes, but I had a tolerant mother—I'm afraid Maureen would never cope with them.'

'But they're not much work, and Paul would look after them. What about a puppy?' she asked, knowing already that it was useless—the governess obviously had the last say in such matters. She fell silent as they walked slowly down a gloomy *steeg*, twisting itself between old houses which had long ago been beautiful but were now let out in rooms. She glanced at the door they were passing, noticing its lovely ruined carving, and at that moment it was flung open and a very small puppy was ejected by a heavy boot. Phoebe had scooped the pitiful object up, hammered on the door with an indignant fist and was actually confronting the dour-looking man who opened it before she was reminded that she would be unable to tell him just what she thought of him. She turned to her companion, her eyes ablaze with indignation, and he gave her a smiling shake of the head and began at once to engage the man in conversation. She couldn't understand a word of it, but the man looked annoyed, frightened and then downright cowed, muttering answers to the questions the doctor was putting to him in his calm, commanding manner. It didn't surprise her in the least that the man, after one final mutter, banged the door and Lucius said on a laugh: 'I feel sure that you are about to tell me that this creature is an answer from heaven, although he is hardly the breed I would have chosen. But it really won't do, you know. Maureen refuses to live in the same house as tame mice, so she will most certainly not agree to a dog—and such a dog!'

Phoebe bit back the forceful things she wished to say about Maureen.

'Oh, please,' she entreated softly, 'couldn't you—just him, not the mice—I'm sure he's a dear little dog and Paul would love him. Look how sweet he is!'

A gross exaggeration, she was aware, as she studied the puny, shivering puppy tucked in her arms. He stared back at her hopefully and heaved a sigh which caused his ribs to start through his deplorable coat. She went on urgently: 'We can't let him go back to that awful man.'

'Set your mind at rest, I have rashly acquired him.'

'Oh, Lucius, you dear!' she burst out, and modified this rash remark with rather stiff thanks and an enquiry as to what was to happen to the animal.

The doctor sighed. 'It just so happens that I have a friend living close by,' he sounded amused and resigned at the same time. 'He is a vet—and don't, I beg of you, tell me that he is an answer from heaven too. I suggest that we take him along now and see what he makes of the little beast.'

They came out of the *steeg* into the Koornmarkt and the vet's house was a bare minute's walk away. He was a man of Lucius' own age and almost as quiet, who listened to Phoebe's earnest explanations, examined the puppy carefully, gave it his opinion that it should do well with proper care and food and bore them both off to drink coffee with his wife while the puppy was taken off to be bathed.

When they left shortly after a brief visit to the now clean animal, Phoebe expressed the view that he was a handsome dog, despite his undernourished frame. She wondered, out loud, what sort of a dog he might be and was indignant when Lucius laughed.

'I shall buy him a collar and a lead,' she declared. 'They will make a birthday present for Paul.' She stopped and turned to look at Lucius. 'You are going to give him to Paul, aren't you?' she asked, suddenly anxious.

He took her arm. 'Of course, but on one condition, that you are at my house by four o'clock tomorrow, for I can see that I shall need all the support I can get when that animal makes his entry.'

# CHAPTER SEVEN

THE tea party was in full swing when Phoebe arrived at the doctor's house the following afternoon. She was surprised to find quite a number of people in the sitting room. Two-thirds of them were children, which was to be expected, the remainder were older people—aunts, uncles and a fair sprinkling of guests whom she had already met or seen in or around the hospital—and of course Maureen. One glimpse of her, in a sleeveless green dress, her hair piled in a cluster of curls, silver sandals on her bare feet, was enough to make Phoebe thankful that she had taken extra pains with her own toilette and had put on a blue silk jersey dress which highlighted her eyes in a most satisfactory manner, and added blue kid sandals to match it. Her hair she had done as she always did, rather severely drawn back from her face, and she wore no jewellery at all. She greeted the doctor sustained by the knowledge that she looked as nice, if not nicer than the governess; the thought added a sparkle to her eye and a faint pink to her cheeks and Lucius, greeting her, paused to take a second look.

'And what have you been up to?' he wanted to know. 'You look—pleased with yourself.'

She looked at him with innocent eyes. 'Me? Nothing—I've been working all the morning.'

She gave him a smile and crossed the room to wish Paul a happy birthday. 'And I've something for you, but I'll give it to you later,' she explained as Arie Lagemaat bore her off to a corner, where he produced tea and cake for her, saying: 'Mies told me to look out for you.'

'If I'd known, I would have changed my off duty so that she could have come—she has far more right to be here than I have.'

He smiled nicely. 'You're mistaken there. I'm waiting for the great moment.'

'Oh—do you know?'

He nodded and smiled as his eyes met hers. 'I'm to tell Mies all about it later.'

'Do you think. . .?' she began, then caught sight of Mijnheer van Vliet, the vet, standing in the doorway. A moment later Lucius crossed the room to where Paul was standing with his own friends. He took the wicker box hesitantly, his eyes on the doctor's face, and then, at the small snuffling sound from it, opened it in a rush. He and the puppy eyed each other for a brief moment and then the boy lifted him out to hold him tight against his chest. 'Is he really for me, Papa?' he asked in a strained little voice.

'Yes, for you, Paul—your very own dog.'

Phoebe thought that Paul was going to burst into tears, but instead he said in an excited voice: 'Oh, Papa, thank you! He's so beautiful and so— so noble—I shall call him Rex.'

As he spoke his eyes slid past Lucius to where Maureen was standing. They held pleading and defiance, but she turned her head away as Lucius went on: 'He's been ill, so I'm afraid Oom Domus will have to take him back for a few more days, but you shall go and see him each day and we'll have him home just as soon as he's fit—and as to thanking me, Paul, it is Phoebe whom you should thank for it was she who begged me to have him—you see, someone had just thrown him out and she rescued him.'

Everyone looked at her so that she smiled in lunatic fashion and retreated as far as possible behind Arie, feeling a fool. But when Paul came across to her, the puppy still clutched close, she forgot about the others. 'You really like him, Paul? I thought he had the sweetest face and such soft eyes. He's going to be happy with you; you'll grow up together.' She produced her own present. 'I thought he might wear these just to begin with, until he's learned to obey you, you know.'

She undid the small parcel for him, because he had no intention of letting go of the dog, and watched while he exclaimed over the red collar and lead.

'I don't know much about dogs,' he told her gruffly as he thanked her.

'Something you'll learn very quickly as you go along,' she assured him comfortably, 'and I'm sure Mijnheer van Vliet will give you lots of good advice, and your papa too.' She stroked the puppy's black nose, 'I'm glad he's made you happy, Paul,' she said.

He turned to go back to his friends and then came close to her to whisper so that she had bend down to hear what he was saying.

'I don't think you're a scheming woman at all—Maureen says I mustn't like you, but I do.'

She said nothing, fearful of breaking the first threads of a friendship which was still too fragile to risk breaking with a careless word. She left soon after that, after a quiet goodbye to Lucius and an exchange of polite words with Maureen, whom, she suspected, was very angry indeed, for as they parted Maureen said with deceptive friendliness: 'You and I must meet some time, Phoebe—I'm sure we have a great deal to say to each other.'

'I'm free on Thursday,' said Phoebe, if she had to grasp the nettle she might as well get it over with, 'can't we meet for tea?'

'My dear, I work, or had you forgotten? But I'll think of something.'

Lucius saw her to the door. On its step he observed blandly: 'I had no idea that you and Maureen were such good friends,' and something in his voice made her look at him sharply, but there was nothing but polite interest in his face.

'We—we know each other very well,' she answered carefully.

He leaned against the heavy door. 'You surprise me. I had quite the reverse impression—which just shows you how unobservant I am.'

She smiled at him. 'Now it's my turn to say I had quite the reverse impression, despite your notebook.'

His hand went to his pocket. 'Good heavens—

wait!' He was thumbing through it. 'I know I made a note—yes, here it is. Have I asked you to dine with me this evening? If not, I'm asking you now.'

She laughed. 'No, you didn't, and if I say yes, will you remember that I did?'

He stared down at her. 'Oh, yes, I shall remember. Thank you for making Paul's birthday such a happy one.'

'It wasn't me—you said yourself that it was an answer from heaven.'

He held her two hands in his, staring down at her, and she wondered what he was going to say. When he spoke she was disappointed.

'*Tot ziens*, then. I'll pick you up at the hospital at eight o'clock.'

It was on her way back that she began to wonder why he wasn't taking Maureen out that evening. She might have another engagement, but she was hardly likely to be pleased if he went off with someone else—perhaps he wasn't going to tell her; perhaps their understanding of each other was so complete that it just didn't matter. If she were Maureen, though, she wouldn't share Lucius with anyone, however platonically.

There was one dress in her wardrobe which she hadn't worn yet, a pastel patterned crêpe. She belted it around her slim waist, caught up a coat and went downstairs as the clock struck eight.

She hadn't given much thought as to where Lucius would take her, for she had been far too excited to think sensibly about anything, and the sight of him, standing on the hospital steps, smoking his pipe and exchanging the time of day with the porter on duty, most effectively splintered the cool she had struggled so hard to maintain.

As they got into the car, Lucius said, 'I thought we'd try Schevingenen——everyone goes there. It's a kind of Dutch Brighton, and if you don't pay it at least one visit, no one will believe you've been to Holland.'

They were out of Delft, streaking down the motorway towards den Haag and the coast, before she said diffidently: 'I thought you would be going out with Paul and Maureen——you know, for a birthday treat.'

He sounded as though he was laughing. 'I took Paul to lunch——Reyndorp's Prinsenhof, I expect you've been there? and we spent the evening at van Vliet's, getting acquainted with Rex. Paul has gone to bed a very happy little boy.'

'I'm glad,' said Phoebe, and wished he would mention Maureen, but he didn't. They entered into a lighthearted conversation about dogs which led, somehow, to talking about her home, and by the time he had parked the car outside the Corvette Restaurant, nothing mattered but the delightful fact that they were to spend the evening together.

It was a gay place and crowded and the menu was enormous. She studied it, hoping for some clue from her companion. It was quickly forthcoming. 'I'm famished,' observed Lucius. 'Paul's idea of lunch is consistent with his age group—*pofferjes*, ice-cream and some mammoth sausage rolls—you see, on his birthday, he plays host and orders the food—I merely eat it.'

Phoebe laughed. 'It sounds frightful, but I expect he loved it and thought you did too.' She added helpfully, 'I'm hungry.'

He sighed with exaggerated relief. 'Good—let's have herring balls with our drinks and then oyster soup, duckling stuffed with apples, and finish with Gateau St Honoré?'

It sounded delicious, although she wasn't sure about the oysters; perhaps they would look different in soup, but by the time they had had their drinks and demolished the herring balls, she was prepared to like anything. Over their meal she found herself telling Lucius exactly why she had taken Sybil's place. 'I thought it was an awful thing to do at first,' she explained a little shyly, 'and then Sybil was so determined to leave, and all the arrangements had been made—and I was longing for a change.' Her voice, without her knowing it, was wistful.

'Ah, yes,' his voice was gentle, 'and to get away from someone, perhaps?'

The excellent Burgundy they had been drinking betrayed her. 'Well, yes, that too—though he did turn up at the wedding.'

Lucius lifted a hand to the waiter and sat back comfortably while the plates were changed. 'And does that mean that there will be more wedding bells?' His tone was so casual that she answered almost without thought.

'Heavens, no! It was just that he was put out

because I didn't fall into his arms like a ripe plum.' She added ingenuously: 'I've forgotten what he looks like.'

'Yes?' he smiled. 'You're more of a peach than a plum, you know. One is sorry for the young man.' He speared a portion of duck. 'But you have another admirer, did you know?'

She kept her eyes on her plate. Maureen or not, had she at last made an impression on his vague abstraction?

'Paul,' he went on cheerfully. 'A bit of a slow starter, wasn't he? But now you're female number one in his world. Maureen had better look out.'

And so had I, thought Phoebe, but all she said was: 'How charming of him. I should like to be friends.'

'Nice of you, Phoebe, after that strange episode in the warehouse. I find it hard to imagine that he did it purely for fun—he must have had some reason.' His eyes searched hers across the table, and silently she agreed with him. Aloud she said comfortably: 'Oh, you know what boys are like, always up to something.' She looked around, desperate to get the conversation on to an impersonal level. 'What a delightful place this is. I expect you come here often.'

His eyes twinkled. 'No—why should I? Only when I'm celebrating something.'

'Paul's birthday; it was kind of you to ask me.'

His lips twitched, but he said no more on the subject, but presently asked her how many more weeks she had in Holland.

'Three—less than that.' She forced her voice to sound cheerful, thinking with dismay that the time was indeed short, and a week of it night duty, too. For the first time for some weeks she wondered what she would do when she got back to England. She might have pursued this melancholy train of thought if her companion hadn't said to surprise her: 'The time has gone very slowly, but probably you haven't found it so.'

Phoebe stared at him, her pretty mouth slightly open. 'No—I haven't. It's all fresh for me and everything's strange, but I expect it's different for you—one nurse after the other coming for a few weeks and then going again. I forget I'm one of a number.'

He didn't answer, only turned as the waiter arrived at the table.

'Ah, here is the famous Gateau St Honoré,' he observed. 'I think it deserves a bottle of champagne, don't you?'

She was on the point of begging him to curb his extravagance, but when she caught the gleam in his eyes, she closed her mouth firmly. Only when the waiter had gone and they were drinking it did he ask her:

'And what were you on the point of saying, dear girl? I have the impression that you disapprove of champagne—surely not?'

'Of course I don't.' She hesitated and went rather red. 'I—I just thought it was—well, champagne is rather expensive—you know, it's for special occasions.'

'You don't consider this a special occasion?'

he was teasing her now. 'Besides, let me set your mind at rest. I have quite enough money to drink champagne with every meal if I should wish to do anything so foolish.'

The red deepened; the knowledge vexed her. 'I beg your pardon,' she said stiffly, 'I had no intention of prying.'

'You're not prying,' he told her placidly. 'I volunteered the information, didn't I? I'm flattered that you were kind enough to consider my pocket—not many girls would.'

The blush which she had succeeded in quenching to some extent returned. 'That's unusual too,' he went on, 'a girl who blushes. Drink your champagne, we're going for a walk.'

They went first to the southern end of the promenade where the fishing harbour, packed with herring boats, lay under the clear evening sky. There was a great deal to see, at least for Phoebe, who found the fishermen's wives in their voluminous dresses and white caps quite fascinating. They lingered there while Lucius explained the variations of costume to her; he explained about the annual race by the herring boats to bring back the first herrings, too, and showing no sign of impatience, answered her fusillade of questions about one thing and another. And when she had seen enough, he took her arm and walked her back, the boulevard on one side, the firm, fine sand and the sea on the other, until they reached the lighthouse at the other end, pausing to examine the obelisk marking the exact spot where William had landed after the Napoleonic wars, and then walked back again.

It was a fine evening, pleasantly warm and fresh after the rain, and there were a great many people about, strolling along arm in arm, just as they were. Phoebe heaved a sigh of content because for the moment at any rate, she was happy, and although she told herself it was probably the champagne, she knew quite well that it was because she was with Lucius. And make the most of it, my girl, she admonished herself silently.

It was dark by the time they got back to the Kurhaus Hotel; strings of lights festooned the boulevard; the café and restaurants still crowded, were ablaze with lights too, and there was music everywhere. It seemed a fitting end to their evening to sit outside the restaurant, looking at the sea and drinking a final cup of coffee, and surprisingly, still with plenty to say to each other, although thinking about it later, Phoebe was forced to admit that she had done most of the talking.

It was midnight when they reached the hospital and when she began a little speech of thanks as they got out of the car Lucius stopped her with: 'No need of thanks, Phoebe. I haven't enjoyed myself so much for a long time—and I'm coming in—I want to have a look at Wil.'

But that didn't stop her from thanking him just the same, once they were in the hospital. The hall porter had his back to them, there was no one else about. Lucius heard her out, clamped her immovable with his hands on her shoulders and kissed her soundly. 'Go to bed,' he said, 'my delightful Miss Brook.'

She didn't see him at all the next day, and when Doctor Pontier came to do a round on the following morning, she asked with careful casualness where he was.

Her companion gave her a quick look. 'The boss is in den Haag,' he told her. 'Some international meeting or other—it lasts three days, I believe. He's there all day; doesn't get home until the evening and leaves again early each morning.'

She murmured something. Lucius hadn't said anything to her when they had been out together, but then, her common sense told her, why should he? She refused an invitation to the cinema, pleading a headache, and went off to cope with little Wil, who was poorly again.

She had just got off duty that afternoon and was on her way up to her room when the warden called after her that there was a young lady to see her. At least Phoebe, understanding only a few words, guessed that was the message. She turned and went downstairs again; it would be Maureen, her instinct warned her—and it was. Phoebe, seeing her sitting there in the comfortable rather drab little sitting room she shared with the other staff nurses, regretted that she had had no warning of her visitor; she would have re-done her face at least and tidied her hair. She said: 'Hullo, Maureen,' and her visitor smiled from her chair and said slowly: 'Hullo. My dear, how frightfully worthy you look in that uniform, though I must say it's a bit ageing—perhaps you're just tired.'

Phoebe sat down in a small overstuffed chair, smiled her acknowledgement of this remark, and waited for Maureen to begin.

'This business with that damned dog—how clever of you, Phoebe. Did you hope to win Paul over to your side because you knew Lucius is soft about him? If you did, you're more of a fool than I thought. What did you hope to gain, I wonder? Lucius? Oh, I've seen your face when you look at him, so don't pretend that you're not interested. But it's no good, my dear, I've got him where I want him—I only have to whistle and he'll come, he and his home and his cars and his lovely bank balance. You see he thinks Paul adores me and he would do anything for the boy.'

'You'll have Paul too,' Phoebe said flatly.

'I've got him where I want him too, so hands off. I must say you've got a nerve, coming here and making doe's eyes at Lucius. And don't think that you've stolen a march on me with your dinners at Schevingenen and your birthday tea parties and your Florence Nightingale act. . .'

'How incredibly vulgar you are!' Phoebe spoke in a cool voice which quite hid her rage, bubbling away inside her and threatening to burst out of her at any moment. 'And do you really suppose that I should listen to you? Why, you don't even like me, and that's good enough reason to take no notice of anything you say.' She got to her feet and walked to the door. 'I'm sorry for Lucius—and Paul.'

In her room she took off her uniform, had a bath and then sat on her bed, having a good cry, which, while playing havoc with her face, did her feelings a great deal of good. She had no intention of heeding Maureen, and what could the girl do anyway? She would have to wait for Lucius to ask her to marry him—Phoebe's heart gave a joyful little bound because he hadn't done that yet, and until then, if Lucius asked her to go out with him again, she would most certainly go. He might not be in love with her, but at least he enjoyed her company, even if she could delay Maureen's plans for another week or two. She closed her eyes on the awful vision of Maureen, married to Lucius—but Lucius might not have made up his mind; he was a deliberate man, not given to impulsive action, at least it was a straw to clutch at.

Phoebe dressed and went down to tea and, carried on the high tide of hope, went out and bought a new dress, something suitable for dinner or an evening out—green and silky and extremely becoming. It was a shocking price; she told herself she was a fool throwing money away on a forlorn hope, but she felt a great deal more cheerful as she left the shop.

She saw Paul the next morning, hurrying along the Koornmarkt. It amused her a little to see how cautiously he looked around him before he crossed the road to speak to her. 'I'm going to see Rex,' he told her. 'I suppose you wouldn't like to come with me?'

Phoebe agreed promptly. The vet's house was close by, and she had half an hour to spare. She occupied the short journey with questions about the puppy and listened to the little boy's happy chatter—Rex was to come home in a day or so, he told her; his papa would be back by then to help him decide where the puppy should sleep and what he should eat and when he should go for his walk. There was no doubt about it, Paul was a changed child, and changed towards her too, for at the vet's door he said in an off-hand voice: 'I'm glad I met you. Maureen won't talk about him, you see, and Else hasn't much time, though she says she'll like to have a dog in the house.'

Mijnheer van Vliet was home. He took them through the surgery to his house where Rex was waiting for them, a very different dog from the miserable little creature she had picked up. He flung himself at Paul and watching them together, Phoebe could only hope that Maureen would relent and at least treat the puppy with kindness even if she disliked it. After all, it would be Paul who would be looking after the dog. She met the vet's eyes and smiled. 'They're made for each other, aren't they? I must go—I'm on duty in an hour.'

She was at the door when Paul ran up to her and said in a conspirator's voice: 'You won't tell Maureen about us coming here, will you?'

'No, dear, not if you don't want me to—

anyway, I seldom see her, do I, so it's not very
likely I should mention it. But why not, Paul?
You're not afraid?'

He wouldn't answer her, but ran back to Rex,
leaving her to wonder if Maureen had forbidden
him to have anything to do with her, but surely
that was a bit high-handed?

The following day was Mies' day off which
meant that Phoebe would have charge of the
ward from two o'clock until the night nurses
came on duty. The ward was quiet when she
took over. There was no one very ill, only little
Wil, sitting in her cot, her small chest labouring,
her face too thin and white. True, she looked no
worse than she had done for several days, but
Phoebe wasn't happy about her. She confided
her opinion to the invaluable Zuster Pets, who,
although she didn't know much about it,
promised to keep a careful watch on the child.

But it was Phoebe who was there when, just
at seven o'clock when the ward was at its busiest,
little Wil collapsed. Doctor Pontier had been to
see her at teatime and although he shared
Phoebe's vague fears, he had been unable to find
anything wrong. Phoebe decided that she was
being over-anxious—all the same, she found
herself taking a look at Wil at more and more
frequent intervals. And lucky for her that she
had, she muttered as she switched on the oxygen,
plugged in the sucker and rang the emergency
bell by the cot. There was no one in the end ward
at that moment. When she heard someone behind
her she said: 'Pets—keep the other children

out and send for Doctor Pontier.'

'Will I do?' Lucius' voice was quiet. She looked over her shoulder at him, unable to keep the joy out of her face or her voice.

'Lucius,' she spoke his name instinctively, and then, remembering where she was, 'Wil has collapsed, sir, she's been off colour all day. Doctor Pontier came to see her at teatime, but he couldn't find anything—a slight temp, but she's had that on and off for a day or two.' She had put a thermometer under Wil's arm and she withdrew it now.

'Forty-point-two centigrade,' she told him, 'and a racing pulse.'

There was no need to tell him the respiration rate, he could see the small heaving chest for himself. He was already sitting on the cot, his stethoscope out, his hands moving quietly over the bony little body. Presently he looked up. 'You know what this is?' he asked.

'Empyema?' she ventured, and glowed at his appreciative nod.

'Good girl, yes—rapid symptoms, I must say, but I'll stake my reputation on it. Let's try an aspiration.'

Zuster Pets had arrived, solid and dependable. Lucius spoke to her and she went away again and he got off the cot and took off his jacket. 'I'll just scrub—stay here, Phoebe, and keep a sharp eye open. We'll need an X-ray—get someone to warn them. Ah, Pontier, just in time. . .' He switched over to his own language and Phoebe, passing on the instructions he had given her, went back to her patient.

The X-ray confirmed the diagnosis; Wil would have to go to theatre and have the cavity drained of the pus which had accumulated there. Phoebe was kept busy for the next half hour getting the small creature ready for the small, vital operation, and when she had seen her safely theatrewards, the faithful Pets in attendance, she applied herself to the preparation of the drainage bottles, the making up of the cot and all the small paraphernalia needed for the night.

Wil was back, perched up against her pillows, when Lucius came in. After he had bent over his small patient he turned to Phoebe. 'Fortunately we were able to tackle it at once—I've rarely seen one with such urgent symptoms—in fact,' he grinned at her, 'I've rarely seen one.'

Phoebe folded a small blanket and hung it over the end of the cot.

'I'm so glad!'

'It was thanks to you, Phoebe. No, I know what you're going to say, but you were quick off the mark. Well, I'm off home, I told them I'd be back an hour ago. Pontier will keep an eye on things.'

He nodded and walked rapidly away, but halfway down the ward he came back again. 'I'm almost sure I've forgotten something—I'll telephone if it's anything important.'

It was Sunday the next day and Phoebe's day off again, and although she had no reason to get up early, she did, because lying in bed was too conducive to thought, and she didn't want to think. She made tea and nibbled toast, then sat on her bed, wondering what to do. The beach would be crowded and it wouldn't be much fun on her own, and the idea of a bus trip didn't appeal. She was looking at her guide book when Zuster Pets knocked on the door. 'There's a telephone call for you,' she declared. 'It's Doctor van Someren.'

Phoebe flew to the telephone. It was Wil, of course—something had gone wrong. She snatched up the receiver and said Hullo in a breathless voice.

'Hullo,' said Lucius in her ear. 'You sound terrified—what's the matter?'

'Wil,' she managed.

'Doing well. Tell me, did I invite you to spend the day with us?'

'No.'

'Ah, then that is what I forgot yesterday evening on the ward. Will you?'

'Well. . .' began Phoebe, disciplining her tongue not to shout an instant yes.

'Good—I'm taking Paul to Noordwijk for a swim, then I thought we might go for a run round for a while. Else has promised us a bumper tea when we get back.'

'Nice! I'd like to, thank you.' Maureen's brilliant image floated before her in the telephone box, but she dismissed it firmly. 'When shall I be ready?'

'Half an hour. We'll pick you up.'

Phoebe dressed like lightning, not bothering with make-up and tying her hair back with a ribbon to match the pink cotton. The half hour was up as she rammed her beach clothes into her shoulder bag.

Paul was sitting in the back with Rex on his knee and there was no sign of Maureen. Phoebe smiled widely at the three of them and got in beside Lucius, who leaned over her to shut the door, remarking: 'Paul was sure you would never be ready—half an hour isn't long.' His gaze swept over her and he smiled nicely. 'But you seem to have made good use of it.'

She flushed faintly and turned to ask Paul about Rex, and the journey to the beach was wholly taken up by a cheerful three-sided conversation about dogs and Rex in particular.

'Is he home for good?' Phoebe wanted to know.

Paul nodded happily. 'Yes, today—we've just fetched him. He'll have all day to get used to being with us before Maureen comes. . .' He broke off and Lucius said mildly:

'Oh, come now, old chap, Maureen will like him, you see if she doesn't, once he's a member of the family. He only needs to learn his manners—she'll be enchanted with him.'

An opinion to which Phoebe found herself unable to subscribe.

The day was an enormous success; it was still too early for the beach to be crowded. They swam, sunbathed, swam again, and then, after Phoebe had made coffee for them all in the chalet and Rex had renewed his energy with a bowl of milk, they got back into the car. An early lunch,

Lucius decreed; they went back inland to Oegsgeest, to de Beukenhof, an inn standing in its own garden and renowned for its cooking. They ate splendidly—Boeuf Stroganoff and strawberries and cream—and Rex, on his best behaviour, sat under Paul's chair.

They went north after that, to Alkmaar and on to den Helder and across the Afsluitdijk, where Lucius, to please Paul, allowed the Jaguar to show a fine burst of speed. But once on the mainland again, he turned off the main road, idling along the dyke roads as far as Lemmer before taking to the main road again, to race across the Noord Oost polder to Kampen and Zwolle and eventually to the motorway to Amsterdam and Delft. Phoebe, trying to see everything at once and failing singularly, found the day passing too quickly. It had been per- fect—Paul was friends at last, Maureen wasn't there with her barbed quips and sly jokes, and Lucius—Lucius was the perfect companion; even if she hadn't loved him she would have allowed him that. True, he was not a man to draw attention to himself in any way, but he had a dry humour which she found delightful and even in the traffic snarl-ups they encountered from time to time, he remained cool and placid, and when the road was free before then, he drove at speed with the same placid coolness. Phoebe sat beside him and thought how wonderful it would be to be married to him—an impossible dream. She shook her head free of it and, obedi- ent to Paul's advice, gazed out of the window at a particularly picturesque windmill.

They had a sumptuous tea in the garden, sitting by the water, all of them talking a great deal and doing full justice to the sandwiches and cakes Else had provided. Phoebe was surprised at Lucius' lighthearted mood. Listening to his mild teasing, she wondered how she could ever have found him absent-minded and vague. Was this his true self, she hazarded, or had he been like this all the time and she hadn't noticed because she had started out expecting him to be exactly as Sybil had described him? She filled the tea cups again, reflecting that it really didn't matter; she loved him whatever he was.

She watched him carry the tea tray back into the house and longed to stay there, in the garden by the water, with the church bells ringing from a dozen churches and Rex snoring on Paul's knee, but she got to her feet as Lucius rejoined them, saying: 'I think I must be getting back— letter to write. . .'

Such a silly excuse, but it would have to do. She failed to see his smile and found it disconcerting when he said at once: 'I'll drop you off— I want to go to St Bonifacius myself.'

It wasn't until he drew up outside its doors and they were walking up the steps together that he said: 'I'll be here at half past seven—will that suit you? We'll find somewhere quiet to have dinner.'

Phoebe stood on the top step, looking up at him, waiting for her heart to slow and give her the breath to speak. 'I'd like that,' she managed, and went across to the Home on wings, for wasn't there a new dress in the cupboard, waiting to be worn?

Before she went to sleep that night, she tried to recall every second of the evening and couldn't—there was too much to remember; the drive along the motorway to Arnhem, and the village—Scherpenzel, such a funny name—where in De Witte Hoelvoet, they had eaten their dinner, not one single item of which could she recall. They had lingered over their meal and it had been late when Lucius stopped the Jaguar outside the hospital once more, and despite her protests had walked into the quiet entrance hall with her and in the centre of its utter quiet, had taken her in his arms and kissed her, and this time he hadn't been in the least vague.

She lay in bed, fighting sleep, thinking about it, and when at last she allowed her eyes to close, she dreamed of him.

# CHAPTER EIGHT

PHOEBE was due for night duty again at the end of the week, and that meant that in no time at all she would be going home. She began, half-heartedly, to think about the future; perhaps it would be a good idea to go right away—Australia perhaps, or Canada. She had always wanted to travel, but now that urge seemed to have left her and the prospect of doing so daunted her. But there were good nursing jobs to be had in either country, although even the other side of the world, she reflected sadly, wasn't far enough away for her to forget Lucius.

She hadn't seen him for two days now. He was at Leyden, Mies had told her, a member of the Board of Examiners at the Academisch Ziekenhuis, adding diffidently that her Arie hoped to be elected to that august body in a few years' time, which remark naturally led the conversation away from Lucius to the fascinating one of her own future.

'We shall marry quite soon,' Mies confided happily, digressing briefly to explain the laws governing marriage in the Netherlands. 'Arie has a good salary and a splendid job and there will be a flat for us. . . I shall not work.' She eyed Phoebe speculatively. 'I do not understand how it is arranged, but why should you not take my

186

place as Hoofd Zuster when I leave? You know the work well and you please Lucius, and if you take lessons you will soon learn Dutch—you are a clever girl.'

The prospect appalled Phoebe. It would be an impossibility to stay in Delft, seeing Lucius every day, but only as his Ward Sister, while Maureen. . . She shuddered delicately. She had done some hard thinking during the last few days; Maureen had told her that she had Lucius just where she wanted him, and although she didn't want to believe it, it was probably true. She was an attractive girl and she knew how to make herself charming, and almost certainly Lucius believed that Paul adored her. Phoebe sighed. How blind could a man be? And he had told her himself that he was going to get married; probably, she thought bitterly, he regarded her as an old friend to whom he could confide his plans.

She ground her excellent teeth and because she didn't want to hurt Mies' feelings, shook her head regretfully.

'It's a lovely idea,' she agreed mendaciously, 'but I don't think it would succeed. For one thing, there must be lots of Dutch nurses with better qualifications than I, who want the job, and for another I doubt if I could get a work permit for an unlimited period.'

Neither of which reasons were insurmountable, but they sounded authentic, because Mies nodded regretfully. 'That is so—a pity. And now that you are here, we will arrange your free days. I have had such a splendid idea. You have but a week of day duty when you come off nights. I will give you only two nights off, the others you shall add to your day off at the end of your last week, thus you will be able to go home three days earlier than you expect.'

She looked so pleased with herself that Phoebe could not but agree with an enthusiasm she didn't feel. She had no wish to go home three days earlier—three days during which she might see Lucius—she had, in fact, no wish to go home at all.

And not only was time growing short, but everything else seemed against her, for the very evening she went on night duty, the weather changed dramatically to a chilling rain and a fierce wind from the sea which, even if Lucius had suggested it, and he hadn't, would have put their morning swim out of the question. Phoebe's hope that the weather would clear in a day or so proved a forlorn one; if anything it became steadily worse, and her temper with it, largely because she never saw Lucius at all—not until her fourth night on duty, and then he was in Maureen's company.

Phoebe had had a busy night, the third of her week's work. She had gone to bed tired and dispirited and quite unable to sleep. After several hours, during which time her thoughts were of no consolation to her at all, she got up, made herself some tea, wrote a letter home and decided that since it was only six o'clock and she had several hours before she needed to go on duty, she might as well go out and post it. A walk would do her good, she told herself, bundling on her raincoat and knotting a scarf under her chin with no thought for her appearance. She was on her way back, feeling hollow-eyed and pale from lack of sleep, when the Jaguar slid past her with Lucius at the wheel and Maureen beside him.

Maureen had seen her. Before Phoebe could cross the road, Lucius, obedient to his companion's direction, pulled the car into the curb.

It was Maureen who opened the conversation. 'My word,' she said in a voice which dripped a bogus sympathy, 'you do look a wreck! Just look at her, Lucius—the poor thing should be in bed—red-rimmed eyes and no colour!'

Phoebe managed a smile in answer to this perfidious attack. 'Oh, we all look like this after a few nights,' she said in a slightly brittle voice. 'You should try it and see.'

Her smile was as brittle as her voice. Probably it looked grotesque on her pallid face—she didn't care; she included Lucius in it just to let him see how fabulous she felt. But it was a useless effort, for he leaned across Maureen and said: 'Phoebe, you look fagged out. Are you all right?'

Before she could reply Maureen's gay voice cut in: 'You look at least thirty, my dear! I had no idea that a few nights out of bed could play such havoc with a girl's looks. You poor dear, going to a hard night's work just as we're starting out to spend our evening. . .'

Phoebe suddenly didn't want to hear how they were going to spend their evening; there was a gap in the traffic. With a hasty: 'I must go, or I shall be late,' she fled across the street.

It was after ten o'clock when Lucius came into the ward. She hadn't expected him, naturally enough—indeed, her evening had been made wretched by the thought of him wining and dining Maureen at some fabulous place, drinking champagne and living it up. She and the student nurse had just finished clearing up the mess after one of the smaller children had been sick. She was going down the ward, wrapped in a plastic apron a good deal too large for her, pushing the runabout full of linen to be sluiced. She eyed him uncertainly, decided that to get rid of the runabout was more important than going to meet him and with a murmured: 'I won't be a moment, sir,' she made for the sluice door. He opened it for her and followed her inside, so that she paused in her tracks and exclaimed in a shocked voice: 'Oh, you mustn't come in here, sir!'

'Why not?' he asked lazily. 'Is it sacrosanct?'

Which despite herself, moved her to hushed laughter. 'Don't be ridiculous! It just isn't—isn't suitable for you. Who did you want to see?'

He shrugged wide shoulders. 'My patients—no hurry. Tell me, Phoebe, do you find night duty too much for you? You looked exhausted this evening. Maureen thought. . .'

It was too much! Phoebe hurled her noisome bundle into the sink and turned on the tap. 'How kind of her to concern herself—I daresay she pointed out my haggard looks with a wealth of detail. I only hope it didn't spoil your evening together.' She turned off the tap with quite unnecessary violence and turned to face him where he lounged against the tiled wall.

He spoke blandly. 'Well, perhaps night duty may not exhaust you, but it certainly sharpens your temper.' He put his hands in his pockets and crossed his legs comfortably. 'As it happens I spent the evening at home—with Paul—and when he had gone to bed, I went to my study and worked, and a good thing I did, it seems, for you appear to grudge me any amusement I may care to arrange for myself.'

There was a wicked gleam in his eye which she ignored. 'I don't!' she declared hotly. 'What about. . .' She was about to remind him of their evening at Schevingenen and the dinner they had had together, but instead she said with a haughtiness which sat ill on her unglamorous appearance: 'I'm not in the least interested in your private life,' and started to tear off her apron. It was a pity that she hadn't thought to take off her rubber gloves first. After watching her wrestling with an ever-tightening knot Lucius offered mildly: 'If you'll turn round, I'll do it.'

She stood, her back like a ramrod, while he worked away at it, and when he had freed her he said in quite a different voice—impersonal, a little cool: 'Good. Now if I might take a quick look at this vomiting infant before I go. . .'

He went shortly afterwards, wishing her a pleasant good night, whistling softly as he went down the stairs. Phoebe, her pen poised over a chart, listened to his footsteps growing fainter and fainter. They seemed symbolic of the future; she closed her eyes on sudden tears and then opened them resolutely and began to write in her neat hand.

It was two mornings later, as she was on her way out for a morning walk before bed, that she was overtaken in the entrance hall by Mies, running and waving an envelope at her.

She thrust it at Phoebe and said, very out of breath: 'I remembered that you said that you would take a walk. These are reports for Doctor van Someren—they came by mistake to the ward, you understand, and he will not be here today—he is at Leyden, but he goes home, I think, and he can see them there. Please to hand them in at his house.' She smiled in her friendly fashion. 'It is no hardship for you to do this?'

'No hardship,' said Phoebe. He wouldn't be home, anyway, so it made no difference at all. She might encounter Maureen, but her mood was such that she really didn't care. Besides, she might just as well walk past his house as anywhere else.

It was another dreary day, but she hardly noticed the fine rain as she walked briskly through the streets, glad to be out in the fresh air after her hectic night, her mind empty of thought because she was tired. She took the shortest way, deciding to go and have coffee at the Prinsenkelder and then go straight back to bed and, she hoped, to sleep.

She could hear Rex yelping as she raised her hand to the heavy knocker on Lucius' door. She heard Maureen's high-pitched voice, shrill with fury, at the same time, and when no one came she tried the door. It opened under her hand and she went in.

Maureen was in the sitting room with her back to the door so that she didn't see Phoebe. She had the dog lead in her hand and cringing on the floor was the terrified Rex. As Phoebe paused in the doorway, appalled, she raised her arm to bring the lead down once more, but this time Phoebe, galvanised into sudden action, caught her arm from behind, wrenched the lead from her and threw it into the corner of the room.

'You're mad!' she declared incredulously, and turned her attention to the puppy. He was shivering, very frightened, and there was a cut over one of his boot-button eyes. He winced and yelped as she lifted him gently to try to discover if he were injured and was relieved to find that at least all four of his legs seemed normal; she had no idea how long Maureen had been beating him, but undoubtedly he was severely bruised, if nothing worse. She laid a soothing hand on his heaving little body and turned to speak to Maureen.

'You must be mad—whatever possessed you, to ill-treat something so small and defenceless— and to hurt Paul? Why did you do it?'

Maureen flung herself into a chair. 'Oh, shut up,' she said roughly. 'Just my filthy luck for Else to go out and leave the door unlocked.

Another few minutes and the little brute would have been dead. Take it away, Miss do-gooder, and I'll think up some tale or other about it running away.'

'You'll break Paul's heart—he loves Rex.'

The other girl laughed. 'Don't be such a fool! Do you think I care about that kid's feelings? Do you imagine that I enjoy being a governess? You're so dim. It serves my purpose, that's all— it keeps me near Lucius.'

Phoebe had gone to sit in a chair with Rex on her lap, examining him more carefully; neither of them heard the street door open, and both of them were taken by surprise when Lucius came into the room, but it was Maureen who recovered first. She was out of her chair in a flash, exclaiming: 'Lucius—thank heaven you've come! I'm in such a state! Rex ran out of the door and got knocked down by a car—Else left the door ajar when she went out. Luckily Phoebe came along with some message or other—I've not had the time to ask her—she's looking to see if he's badly hurt.' This remarkable speech had the effect of rendering Phoebe speechless. She gave Maureen an incredulous look and turned to Lucius, but he wasn't looking at either of them; he was bending over the puppy, examining him in his turn. Phoebe, seething with unspoken words, bit them back; a row wouldn't help Rex, for it would waste time. She said quickly: 'I hope he's not badly hurt.'

'It's hard to tell, but I don't think so. Probably the edge of the pavement or a stone cut his eyelid;

he must have been tossed clear. Did the car stop?' He glanced briefly at Maureen.

'No—I didn't actually see it happen, only heard the noise—poor little beast.' Her voice was warmly sympathetic as she started to cross the floor towards them. 'I'll take him round to the vet—I can take the Mini. . .'

Phoebe caught her breath. 'No,' she said more sharply than she intended, 'I'll take him. Mijnheer van Vliet's house is close by—I'll carry Rex.'

There was a short pause until Lucius said deliberately: 'Thank you, but I shall take him myself and I'll pick up Paul from school at midday and take him along to see how Rex is shaping.' He picked up the puppy and started for the door and paused to ask of Phoebe: 'Why did you come?'

'I was asked to deliver some reports. I put them on the table in the hall.'

He nodded: 'Thanks,' and shut the door quietly behind him. There was silence after he had gone. Presently Phoebe left the house too, not speaking at all to Maureen, for she could think of nothing that she could say which might improve matters, and if she uttered the things she wanted to, it would probably make things hard for Paul as well as Rex. Besides, there was the chance that Maureen, after such a narrow shave, might change her ways. Phoebe hurried through the rain, wondering if and how she should tell Lucius about it and would he believe her if she did? Maureen was a clever girl, she would be able to turn a situation, however adverse to herself, to good advantage. Phoebe decided to wait until she was on the point of leaving Holland—only a few days away now. She would tell Lucius then and it would be up to him to sort things out for himself. She had forgotten her coffee. She walked around the streets aimlessly and was on her way back to the hospital when she suddenly decided to go and see Mijnheer van Vliet.

He received her very kindly and led her at once to the room at the back of the surgery where the sick animals were housed. Rex, looking sorry for himself, was in a basket, still shivering, but he opened one eye and looked at her warily and essayed to wag his tail.

'How is he?' asked Phoebe anxiously.

'He'll recover,' the vet smiled at her. 'He's a tough little chap—a few days and he'll be well again.' He added on a puzzled note: 'Only his injuries do not match up with a car accident. I am a little perplexed. . .'

'Look,' said Phoebe earnestly, wondering why she hadn't thought of telling him in the first place, 'it wasn't a car. I know how it happened, but you mustn't tell anyone—you'll understand why.'

She plunged into her tale, and when she had finished, Mijnheer van Vliet nodded his head. 'So that is the story, and a shocking one, but I must tell you that I am not altogether surprised. For some reason Maureen promised—oh, a couple of years ago, that she would give Paul a puppy. Always there have been reasons why she has not done so—it is as if she punishes him by refusing his constant wish to have a dog—and now he has Rex, a dog which she has not given him, and she is angry. I do not understand, but I thank you for telling me. I will say nothing, of course, but I promise you that I will keep an eye on him—daily visits perhaps, a check-up each week, something—and until then I will keep him safe here with me.' He eyed her thoughtfully. 'You do not feel that you should tell Lucius?'

She blinked her beautiful eyes in deep thought. 'No—you see Lucius thinks that Maureen is kind and good for Paul and that he's fond of her, and perhaps that is the truth—I don't know. Besides,' she paused, seeking the right words, 'they have known each other a long time, Lucius and Maureen. They're—they're old friends.'

Mijnheer van Vliet growled deeply, coughed hugely and offered her coffee, making no comment. She refused the coffee, saying that she really would have to get back to the hospital and get some sleep, and after a final look at Rex, she walked back to the Home, too tired by now to think sensibly about anything, and as it turned out, too tired to sleep.

She went on duty looking distinctly haggard and not much caring. The ward was busy, there was a great deal to do, and it was almost one o'clock in the morning when she sat down at her desk in the now quiet ward and a few minutes later Lucius came, looking vast in the dim, shadowed surroundings. Phoebe got to her feet wearily and wished him good evening, and he said softly:

'Hullo, Phoebe—they're all OK, aren't they? I came to see you to tell you that Rex is better. He's to stay with van Vliet for a day or two.'

'And Paul?'

'He was upset, but he feels better now he's seen him.' He leaned over and turned the desk lamp on to her face. 'You've not slept,' he stated baldly, and then, to take her breath: 'What was wrong this morning?'

She faltered a little: 'Wrong? What do you mean?'

His voice was bland. 'You and Maureen. But I see you have no intention of telling me.'

'No.'

He nodded to himself. 'A little tiff, I suppose—you were tired, weren't you, and I daresay, short-tempered, and Maureen is no good with animals. She finds them a nuisance even when she wants to help them. I daresay you arrived just in time to prevent her having hysterics.'

Phoebe eyed him unsmilingly; he had called her short-tempered and somehow put her in the wrong. Well, let him find out for himself. 'You might say that,' she told him.

Lucius turned to go. 'Oh, Paul sent his love. He hopes you will go and see Rex.'

'Of course I will. Please give him my love.'

He lingered. 'You're friends at last. I wonder what stood in the way when you first met?'

She returned his thoughtful stare. 'I have no idea. Good night, sir.'

His lips twitched, he gave her a mocking smile. 'Good night, Nurse Brook.'

She went the following morning to see Rex and this time stayed for coffee with Mijnheer van Vliet and his wife. 'Rex is better,' the vet told her, 'but he's got some brutal weals on his back, poor little beast. He's on penicillin and he eats like a horse. Have you seen Lucius?'

'Yes—on the ward.'

'You didn't tell him?'

'No, and I don't intend to.' She got to her feet. 'Thank you for the coffee. May I come and see Rex again? When is he going home?'

Mijnheer van Vliet laughed. 'Tomorrow or the day after. Paul is longing to look after him and I find it hard to imagine that Maureen will repeat her actions.' He smiled grimly. 'If she does, then whatever you feel, I shall tell Lucius myself and he can find himself another governess.' He walked to the door with her. 'You will be back in England very soon, I understand. I am sorry to hear that; we shall miss you.'

Phoebe sped back to the hospital, wondering if Lucius would miss her too, or if he would forget about her going until she had gone and then wonder where she was.

She hoped that he would visit the ward that night, but this time it was Doctor Pontier. He wrote up a few charts, signed a couple of forms, asked her when she was leaving, hoped for the pleasure of taking her out before she did, and took himself off. He was a nice man, although he had a roving eye. Phoebe thought about him for perhaps ten seconds and then plunged back into her work.

She was late off duty in the morning. Everything had gone wrong—broken thermometers, cross children who refused to be washed, crosser ones who spat out their medicine and the cheerful ones who thought it fun to hide under the bedclothes and have a good romp before being hurried off to clean their teeth and wash their faces. Phoebe, a calm girl when it came to her work, took it all in good part, but by the time she left the ward she was tired enough to go straight to bed.

Breakfast, she promised herself as she went slowly to the dining room, and then a bath and bed. She had done the last night of her duty; she had two days off, so she would sleep until the afternoon, get up, have a walk and go back to bed again. The dining room was almost empty. Phoebe poured coffee, buttered some bread and sat down. She was half way through the coffee when she was told that there was someone to see her and it was urgent. She trailed up the stairs again—the ward had been all right when she left it. It wouldn't be Lucius in this weather; perhaps it was Rex—she hurried her lagging feet as she reached the entrance hall. Paul was there. He looked small and forlorn and wildly angry, and forgetting her tiredness Phoebe hurried to him.

'Paul—what's the matter? Rex?'

He stared at her for a moment and then began

to pour out his tale, becoming quite incoherent and mixing Dutch and English together so that she was hard put to understand him. When he had finished she said in a calm voice: 'Let me get this straight, Paul—you stop me if I go wrong. Your father's away in England—for how long? Two days. He fetched Rex back last night so that you should have him while he was away and this morning Maureen took him and shut him in the shed at the bottom of the garden, and made you go to school—how did she make you, my dear?'

Tears clogged his voice. 'She said it would be the worse for Rex if I didn't—that Papa had told her to do it, but I don't believe her. She's going to hurt him, I know she is.' He fixed her with a pleading eye. 'You must help me, please, Phoebe!'

'Yes, dear, of course I'll help you.'

His face brightened a little. 'You believe me, then?'

'Yes, of course I do. Where are Else and that girl who comes in the mornings?'

'Maureen told them they could have the day off. She does that when Papa's away—she tells them that he has said so, but he hasn't.'

She could well believe that. 'Any ideas?' she asked.

'Could we rescue Rex and run away, just till Papa comes home?'

She considered the idea. 'Is Maureen in the house?'

'Yes, she has friends in when Papa is away.'

She would! thought Phoebe savagely; there were a number of questions she was going to ask, but not now. 'So she wouldn't notice if we slipped into the garden?'

He was quick. 'From the canal. Oh, Phoebe, how clever you are! I can borrow Jan Schipper's boat, he lives a little further along—no one will see us, they'll be in the sitting room.'

'Good, though we must be careful. We'll go now, just as soon as I've changed.' She paused, struck by a thought. 'Where can we go to?'

Paul put a hand to his mouth, his eyes huge above it. 'I don't know,' he mumbled. 'Oom Domus—but he's going to den Haag.'

'Think of someone!' Phoebe besought him. 'Aunts, uncles, friends, an old nanny. . .' He wouldn't know what an old nanny was—but he did.

He said at once: 'Papa's old nanny, Anna, she lives in Amsterdam, I know where. She loves him, she told me so.' He smiled. 'She'll help.'

Phoebe released a held breath. 'Good boy! Sit here and don't move. I'll be ten minutes.'

She was back in seven exactly, not perhaps looking her best, for she had flung on a cotton dress, belted her raincoat over it, concealed her untidy head under a scarf, caught up her shoulder bag, stuffed with a few necessities for the night and all the money she possessed, and raced downstairs again, full of false energy, her sapphire eyes blazing in a washed-out face.

'What about school?' she asked as they raced through the small back streets. When he told her simply that he hadn't been she forbore to say anything. Probably later on she would regret this whole business, but she could think of nothing else and she felt partly to blame because she hadn't told Lucius about the beating Rex had had. She thanked heaven silently that she had nights off and was free to do what she liked.

They came out into the street where Lucius lived, but at its other end, and Paul led her down a narrow dark path between two houses, opened the wooden door at its end and entered a garden. Phoebe hesitated.

'Paul,' she whispered, looking apprehensively over her shoulder at the house beyond the well-kept lawn, 'isn't this private?'

'It's Jan's home, and he's at school. No one will see us, and he won't mind.'

They had reached a small jetty, just like the one in Lucius' garden, and Paul got into the small boat tied to its side. Phoebe got in too; she wasn't sure about Dutch law, but she had a nasty feeling that they could be accused of stealing. 'Undo the rope,' Paul told her. He had the oars out and was already swinging the boat outwards. She did as she was bidden, recognising that he was leading the expedition for the moment, not she. She crouched opposite him, averting her eyes from the houses they were passing. Any moment now, she thought guiltily, some worthy citizen would fling open a window and cry the Dutch equivalent of 'Stop, thief!' But no one saw them. Paul shipped an oar and gentled the boat into the bank. They were there; Lucius' garden, bright with flowers, its beautifully tended lawn shining wetly in the rain, lay before them, and from the shed close at hand came a soft, hopeless whimper.

'I'll get him,' said Phoebe. 'Keep the boat close in, so we can run for it. If anyone comes you're to go on your own with Rex.' She pulled some notes from her bag. 'There, I expect this is enough to get you to Amsterdam.' She gave him a cheerful wink and stepped on to the jetty.

The shed door was fastened from the outside but not locked, which was a good thing because she had no idea what she would have done if that had been the case. Rex was tied up inside and whimpered joyfully when he saw her, but she said 'Hush!' in such an urgent voice that he kept quiet while she sawed through the rope with a pair of blunt garden shears. The simple task took an age. With her heart in her mouth Phoebe picked him up and made for the boat, and once there she had to put a hand over the puppy's muzzle to stop his ecstatic greeting of his young master. 'For heaven's sake,' she said, very much on edge, 'row—you can say hullo to each other presently.'

The return journey wasn't as bad as she had expected it would be; perhaps she was becoming inured to crime. She chuckled at the idea and Paul turned round to say: 'You are what Papa calls a good sport, I think, Phoebe.' Well, he wouldn't think that of her now. She handed the puppy to her companion and he asked: 'What do we do now?'

'The station,' she told him, 'and let's keep off the main streets.'

It was still early as they boarded an Amsterdam train, but the morning rush was over. They sat opposite each other, drinking coffee and eating the rolls Phoebe had bought and sharing them with the puppy. Finally, the last of the crumbs tidied away, Phoebe leaned forward.

'Now, Paul,' she said urgently, 'there are some things I must know.' And when he nodded, she went on: 'Tell me about Maureen, my dear.' She searched his solemn little face. 'There's something...you have always been so careful to be obedient to her and yet I have the idea that you are afraid of her, but if that is so, why didn't you tell your papa?'

He took a deep breath. 'She said that if I did everything she said and——and liked her, she would buy me a puppy; she said it all depended on me whether I had him or not, because she would have to marry Papa before she could get him and if she went away and he had another governess for me she would be old and horrid and I'd never get a puppy of my own; she said,' he gulped, 'that if I said anything to Papa I'd never have anything, not as long as I lived.'

'Is that why you shut me up, Paul?'

He nodded. 'She said that you were a——a menace——that you wanted to marry Papa. Do you?'

Phoebe stared back into his questioning eyes. 'Yes,' she said quietly, 'I do, but you need not worry, your Papa doesn't want to marry me.'

'She said you'd make him.'

She gave a lop-sided smile. 'How, I wonder? Even if I knew, I wouldn't do that, Paul.'

'She said you were a—a—canting hypocrite and a scheming old maid.' He smiled suddenly and endearingly. 'But she's wrong, you're not— I like you. She said I was to hate you, but I don't.' He looked, for a brief moment, forlorn. 'You're a little like my mama.'

She said steadily: 'Am I, dear? I think that's one of the nicest things anyone has ever said to me.' She smiled warmly at him. 'So now we know why Maureen was so angry that you have been given Rex—she has no hold on you any more.'

He didn't quite understand her. 'She said that Rex would die anyway because he was only a street dog, and when he did, she would buy me another, but only if she married Papa.'

'Oh, my dear,' cried Phoebe, 'I often wondered—most people have cats and dogs and a few tame mice or a hamster. . .'

His eyes sparkled. 'I like kittens too, but Maureen said they're not healthy.'

'Oh, pooh,' said Phoebe roundly. 'We've got cats and dogs and they're a great deal more healthy than some people I know.'

'Have you any mice?'

'Well, no—girls don't like mice, you know, but I can see that they make splendid pets for boys.'

She glanced out of the window and suddenly remembered where they were and what they were doing. 'We're almost in Amsterdam; you take Rex, and I'll get a taxi.'

Anna lived in a long street called Overtoom. It was neither picturesque nor in a particularly good part of the city and in the rain any charm it might possess had been obliterated by the greyness of the sky and the dampness of its pavements, but to Phoebe it represented a solution, temporary at any rate, of their most pressing problems. She followed Paul down a flight of stone steps to Anna's front door, just below street level, and waited while he rang the bell.

There was no mistaking Anna when she opened the door, for she was exactly what anyone would imagine an old nanny to be, with bright blue eyes, extremely neat hair parted in the centre and gathered into a bun, and a small round person clothed in a black dress almost completely covered in an old-fashioned print pinny. At the sight of Paul she broke at once into delighted speech and after a minute Paul, remembering his manners, introduced them and said: 'Anna says we're to go inside.'

The rooms were very small and crowded with furniture, all very highly polished, and there was a lovely smell of coffee in the kitchen where Anna bade them sit down at the table. Over their elevenses Paul told his tale, and Phoebe, watching anxiously, was vastly relieved when at the end of it and after a few brisk remarks from Anna, Paul told her:

'Anna says we are to stay here until Papa

comes back, and she's glad we came. You're to sleep on the landing, if you don't mind, because there's only one bedroom and I'm to sleep on the floor—I'll like that, and I'll have Rex.'

Phoebe eyed him tiredly. How resilient little boys were! She felt exhausted herself and said a little desperately: 'Will you tell Anna that I'll telephone your papa as soon as he gets back—in the afternoon. You'll be all right once he's home again, and Paul, do you think Anna would mind if I went to sleep for a little while? I can't keep my eyes open.'

'Oh, Phoebe, I forgot, you've been awake all night.' He addressed himself to the old lady, who peered across the table at Phoebe and nodded her head.

'You're to go to bed now,' Paul told her. 'Anna says you are a sensible girl but that you must have your sleep. You won't be too long?' He sounded wistful.

She shook her head, resolutely ignoring the longing to sleep the clock round. 'An hour or two. Paul, stay indoors, won't you? Is there a yard or something for Rex?'

'A little garden with a high wall,' he told her. She went up three or four steps leading out of the kitchen, guided by Anna, on to a small landing, bare save for a folding bed in one corner and a chair. She smiled sleepily at her kind hostess, tossed her things on to the chair, kicked off her shoes and curled up on the bed. She was asleep within seconds.

It was Paul who wakened her a few hours later,

Rex still tucked under his arm. 'It's teatime,' he informed her. 'Didn't you undress? You must have been sleepy.'

Phoebe yawned, feeling heavy-eyed and hollow, fighting a desire to fall back on the bed again and sleep for ever. 'I was. I say, Paul, I want to wash—is there a bathroom?'

He shook his head. 'You use the kitchen sink. We won't look,' he added kindly as he went away. He was whistling cheerfully and a little off key and Phoebe smiled to herself. At least one of them was enjoying himself!

The remainder of the day passed surprisingly quickly. She tried out a little of her Dutch on Anna, and with Paul's help, they had quite a conversation, and even if they didn't understand each other very well, it didn't seem to matter. Anna, Phoebe could tell, was most definitely on their side, and Phoebe, waking in the night because the mattress wasn't all that comfortable, at least had the satisfaction of knowing that Anna approved of what she had done, she only hoped that Lucius would be of the same opinion.

# CHAPTER NINE

THE rain had eased up in the morning and over their simple breakfast Phoebe discovered that there was a park behind Anna's flat—Vondel Park. It would be a good place to go, she decided as she helped Anna with the washing up. They had to spend the day somewhere until it was time for her to telephone Lucius, and it wasn't fair on Anna to fill her little home to overflowing with a high-spirited small boy and a puppy. They set off presently, with a ball Anna had found from somewhere or other, and strict instructions to be back for their dinner at midday.

The park was pleasant, well laid out and almost empty of people. They walked for a little while, Rex lying snugly in Paul's arms, because, as Phoebe pointed out in her sensible way, they would play ball presently and he would want to join in and he ought not to get too tired.

They had been tossing the ball to and fro for perhaps ten minutes when Paul gave a sudden shout, hurled the ball wildly in the air and started to run towards Phoebe, yelling as he came, his whole face alight with happiness. She spun round, certain who it was she would see—and she was right. Lucius, the ball in his hand, was coming towards them over the grass. He paused to put a hand briefly on Paul's shoulder as they met and then came to a halt before her.

'Don't dare to be angry with him,' she said impulsively, then wished she hadn't spoken, because he was indeed angry, but with her, not Paul. His words bore this out, for when he spoke it was in a silky voice which menaced her far more than a shout.

'I should like to wring your pretty neck,' he gritted. 'How dare you, Phoebe? Such a petty act, it wasn't worthy of you.'

She steadied her shaking mouth. 'But you're back a day too soon. . .'

His eyes blazed. 'And how fortunate that I am—you had overlooked that possibility.' He smiled, not at all nicely. 'I am at a loss to discover why you should have done this—why should you wish to set Paul against Maureen? She telephoned me in great distress—she imagined that you were friendly towards her, so naturally she feels deeply hurt.'

Phoebe found her voice, keeping it low so that Paul, playing with Rex close by, shouldn't hear. 'Is that what she said?' She was surprised at the mildness of her tone; she felt as though she would blow sky-high with rage.

'Yes. When I returned last night I found a note from her asking me to telephone. She told me then that Paul had disappeared.'

'How did she know that I was with Paul?'

'She had the good sense to telephone the hospital and put two and two together.'

'And how,' went on Phoebe stubbornly, 'did you know where we were?'

'Van Vliet suggested I should try Anna—he remembered that Paul had been talking about her.' He added wearily, 'I tried everywhere else last night.'

'Is Maureen at your house?'

He raised his eyebrows. 'No—why do you ask? She will be there by the time we get back, I imagine. But don't worry, I have no intention of reproving you until we have got to the bottom of this in a rational manner, I'm sure that the three of us can discuss. . .'

'I won't,' said Phoebe, in far too loud a voice. 'I'll discuss nothing. You can think what you like, what do I care? You're so completely under that woman's thumb. . .' She stopped, choked and walked away very fast. By the time Lucius, with Paul and Rex, had arrived at Anna's house, she had dried her angry tears, composed her face and was ready with a polite refusal when he offered her a lift back to Delft. And when Paul, aware that something was not right in his little world, began his own muddled explanation, she bade him urgently to be quiet.

'Wait, my dear,' she besought him. 'It won't help now, and it doesn't matter any more, because your Papa is back home, don't you see? Besides, explaining things is so tedious.'

He eyed her. 'You've been crying. I'm sorry I shut you in that house.'

She bent and kissed him. 'I'm going to have a lovely day shopping,' she told him. 'If I see anything for Rex, I shall buy it.'

'The Bijenkorf has some tartan collars with a

silver plate on them, for his name, you know—
they put it on while you wait. . .'

She smiled at him. 'Then that's what I'll get.
Now go back to your father, Paul, he'll be waiting for you.'

He lingered by her. 'You'll come back, won't
you? Won't you come with me to the door? You
haven't said goodbye to Rex.'

Phoebe couldn't refuse him, so she tickled
Rex under his chin, wished Paul a warm farewell
and Lucius a glacial one, and went back to the
landing, where she sat down on the bed, doing
nothing until she heard the door close and knew
that they had gone.

She waited a little while, trying to suppress
the ridiculous hope that Lucius would come
back, and when a half hour had gone by, and she
knew that he wasn't going to, she tidied herself,
stuffed her bag with her bits and pieces once
more and went down to the kitchen to wish Anna
goodbye.

The old lady was sitting at the table, knitting,
but she got up when she saw Phoebe and without
saying a word, drew her through a door into what
must have been the parlour, seldom used and so
stiffly furnished that it reminded Phoebe of a
child's drawing. There was an old-fashioned
sideboard against one wall, dominating the room
and loaded with photos in heavy frames. Anna
picked one up and handed it to Phoebe. It was
Lucius as a small boy, leaning against his
father's knee, a hand on his mother's arm. There
was a baby too, invisible in a lacy shawl, and

another small boy, younger than Lucius, sitting on the floor. She looked at Anna, who smiled and nodded and handed her a quite small photograph—Lucius in a student's gown, looking vaguely at the camera as though his thoughts were far away, and the last one, Lucius, older still, standing with a group of earnest-looking men outside the hospital. Phoebe gave that one back too and her companion put them carefully in their places and led her out again. At the door she took Phoebe's hand in her own and patted it, nodding her head in a satisfied way and murmuring to herself with an air of great content. Phoebe, not having the least idea what she was saying, could only nod and smile, and finally wish her goodbye.

The day stretched before her and she would have to fill it somehow. She would stay in Amsterdam until the evening and then go straight back to the Nurses' Home and to bed. She was on duty early the following morning, and in four days she would be able to go back home. She need not see Lucius again—there were ways of avoiding him on the ward. This firm resolution was instantly followed by a variety of reasons requiring her to seek him out. She could explain, she told herself, walking briskly along Ovetoom, and knew she never would. He had believed Maureen—he hadn't even asked her why they had come to Anna's, although to be fair, she hadn't given him much opportunity. She scowled fiercely and a meek-looking man coming towards her sidled past, looking quite apprehensive. 'Fool!' she said aloud, meaning herself, and found that she had arrived at the Leidseplein.

She wandered along, staring into the shops, stopping at a coffee bar, where she had hard work in repelling the advances of a cheerful young man who was apparently much taken with her looks. He told her so, in English, after she had informed him coldly that she couldn't understand Dutch. It took determination to shake him off. Phoebe plunged into Vroom and Dreesman, at the bottom of the Kalverstraat, going through its departments without seeing anything of them. By now they would be back in Delft. She pictured them sitting in his lovely house, discussing her; Maureen at her most charming, cleverly putting spokes in Paul's small, futile wheel. Well, it wasn't her business any more, only before she left Delft, she would go and see Mijnheer van Vliet and make sure that he did something about Rex—perhaps he could tell Lucius once she had gone—in the nicest possible way, of course.

Phoebe wandered on again and in company with dozens of other women, lunched in the balcony restaurant of the Bijenkorf. It was a nice store, she decided, so she would spend an hour or so exploring its departments, have tea, and then catch a train. It wouldn't matter if she went to bed early; heaven knew she was tired enough.

She was in the kitchenware department, studying a colourful display of saucepans, when she became aware that Lucius was standing beside her, so close that the sleeve of his jacket brushed her arm. A tide of feeling rushed over her; it was ridiculous that his presence beside her should have the power to melt all her carefully built-up resentment, her unhappiness even; to give her an overwhelming desire to cast herself into his arms, whatever he thought of her. Unable to bear it a moment longer, she snatched up a saucepan and studied it with all the interest of a good housewife on the lookout for a bargain. 'Go away!' she said fiercely.

She had lifted the lid and was peering inside when Lucius took it from her with the utmost gentleness and put it down.

'Phoebe, we must talk.' His voice was harsh and urgent.

She wasn't a girl to give in at the drop of a hat. She picked up a small steel object and gave it her full attention. He took that from her too. 'A hard-boiled egg slicer,' he remarked blandly. 'I imagine it to be a useful kitchen tool.'

'Hard-boiled eggs should be sliced by hand,' Phoebe snapped, aware that the conversation, such as it was, was leading them nowhere.

'Indeed? I'm sure you are right.' She thought she detected laughter in his voice now. 'May we talk?'

'No,' said Phoebe coldly. 'I've nothing to say to you.'

'Good, for I have a great deal to say to you.'

'I shan't listen,' she told him defiantly, and shot him a furious glance.

'Yes, you shall listen, my darling heart. I was angry this morning. . .'

Her mind registered the glorious fact that he had called her his darling heart even while she said in a voice squeaky with indignation: 'Angry? You wanted to wring my neck!'

'Your lovely neck,' he corrected her, 'and now listen to me so that you will understand why I was angry. When I got home and found Maureen's note and heard what she had to say on the telephone, I lost my temper—I don't often do that, Phoebe, but you see while I had been in England I had dreamed—oh, a great many dreams—of you, of course, and then when Maureen told me that you had made it up with this young doctor in England and pointed out that you were so very English and I was so very Dutch—and wrapped up in my work, and perhaps a little old—it seemed to me that I had dreamed too much.' He turned to look at her. 'It was like coming back to a nightmare—you gone, Paul gone. I could think of nothing else, and then I found you and I remembered the young doctor.'

'And you wanted to wring my neck—well, of all the. . .!' She paused: a saleswoman, a hawk-eyed, bustling woman, was peering at them from the other side of the saucepans, her dark eyes suspicious. She gave Phoebe a sharp glance and spoke to Lucius, who spoke to her in a smooth voice and actually made her laugh. When she had gone, Phoebe demanded:

'What did you say?'

'She suspected us of being shoplifters, I imagine. I told her that as a young wife, setting up house, you needed time to decide upon your purchases.'

Phoebe chuckled, quite forgetting that they were in the middle of a quarrel. 'Oh, Lucius, how could you? Now I'll have to buy something.'

'Buy anything you wish, my darling, only let me have my say. You see, Paul told me everything on the way back to Delft. I never knew, never even guessed—why didn't you tell me? I can understand why Paul was afraid to tell me, but you—surely you could have said?'

She stared hard at a shelf loaded with frying pans, blinking back sudden tears. 'Maureen said that she was going to marry you and I didn't know if—if you loved her, so I couldn't say anything, could I?' She sniffed and looked at him and away again. 'Maureen said. . .' she began again.

'My dearest dear, have we not had enough of Maureen? You seem obsessed by her, which I assure you I am not. She was Paul's governess, that was all. I found her good at the job. I thought, heaven help me, that he liked her, that she was kind to him—that was why I allowed her to do much as she wished. It seemed to me that his happiness was more important than the unwelcome visitors she sometimes invited into my house, but once and for all, my darling, I must tell you that never once did I contemplate marrying her.'

He turned her round to face him and said gravely: 'I may be absent-minded and perhaps a little blind to what is going on around me, but

there are some things of which I am very sure—
my love for you, Phoebe; you are my life and
my future. Do you suppose you could surmount
the difficulties of marrying a Dutchman and bear
with my occasional lapses of memory? Will you
marry me, my darling?'

'How do you know I'm not going to
marry Jack?'

'Paul told me.'

She leaned back a little against his arm and
stared up into his face. 'But he doesn't know
anything about him.'

'Naturally not, but you told Paul that you
wanted to marry me.'

She drew an indignant breath. 'Well, really—
the little horror! Just wait until I see him!'

She felt Lucius shake with silent laughter.
'You won't get a word in edgeways, my dearest.
He was so excited when I told him that I was
coming back to fetch you. He babbled about
kittens and mice, he even offered, once he has a
cat or so to keep Rex company, to welcome a
brother or sister into the family.'

'Oh, Lucius, darling Lucius, I'll marry you.'
His arms tightened around her, his face was very
close, but she held him away. 'No—no, just a
minute, Lucius, I know we're not going to talk
about Maureen any more, but where is she—did
you see her—I. . .'

'Gone. I had a talk with her when we got back,
and she left the house for good, my darling. And
now don't interrupt me again.'

'You can't—not here—people,' said Phoebe.

He kissed her silent, and when presently she had her breath back and began: 'I don't think. . .' he said comfortably: 'Quite right, my darling, there is no need,' and kissed her again.

In the car on the way to Delft she said shyly: 'I don't know anything about you, Lucius. Anna showed me some photos of you—have you a family?'

'A sister,' he told her, 'married to a Norwegian, a brother living in Canada. My parents are visiting him.'

'Oh—they live here, in Holland?'

'In Friesland—Father is a doctor too. They'll love you, my Phoebe.'

'I hope so. When will they be back?'

'Not for some months. We shall be an old married couple by then.' He drew up before his house and turned to smile at her. 'I told you that I had had dreams while I was in England; they seemed so real that I set about the business of getting a special licence. We can be married very soon, Phoebe.'

She smiled slowly. 'Perhaps that would be a good idea—if we don't get married quickly you might forget.'

They were standing outside the door when she asked: 'Lucius, when we met—you know, in England—you wrote something in your note-book and you looked at me. What was it?'

For answer he took the little leather-bound book from a pocket, leafed through it, found what he sought and handed it to her. The writing was in Dutch, in his neat, rather spidery hand.

Phoebe had picked up quite a vocabulary by now, so had little difficulty in reading it.

'A darling English girl,' she read aloud slowly. 'I shall marry her.'

She closed the book gently and looked up into his face, his kind and loving face, his blue eyes very clear and steady. They would be very happy, she was quite sure of that. She said softly: 'Oh, Lucius, I do love you,' and saw the answer in his eyes before he turned away to unlock the door.

*Harlequin Romance*

**D**elightful

**A**ffectionate

**R**omantic

**E**motional

**T**ender

**O**riginal

**D**aring

**R**iveting

**E**nchanting

**A**dventurous

**M**oving

Harlequin Romance—the
series that has it all!

HROM-G

# HARLEQUIN PRESENTS®

**HARLEQUIN PRESENTS**
men you won't be able to resist falling in love with...

**HARLEQUIN PRESENTS**
women who have feelings just like your own...

**HARLEQUIN PRESENTS**
powerful passion in exotic international settings...

**HARLEQUIN PRESENTS**
intense, dramatic stories that will keep you turning
to the very last page...

**HARLEQUIN PRESENTS**
The world's bestselling romance series!